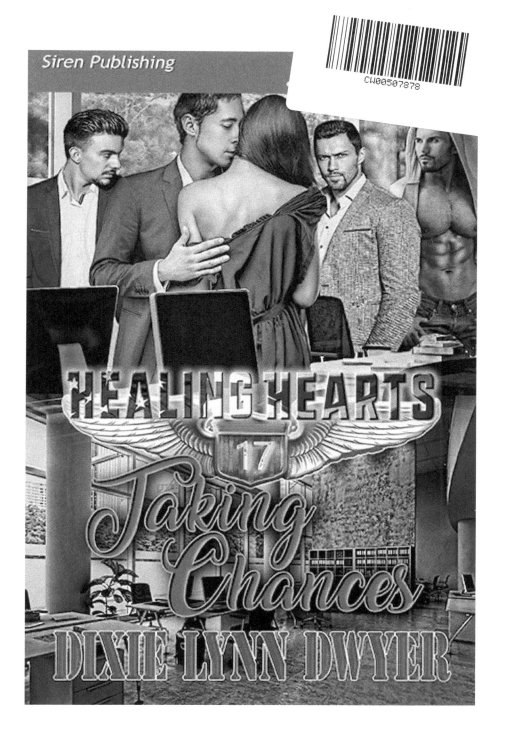

Siren Publishing

HEALING HEARTS

17

Taking Chances

DIXIE LYNN DWYER

Healing Hearts 17: Taking Chances

Melise has a full plate and is just trying to help her family and keep a steady income, the last place she needs to be is in the middle of some criminal gangster activity. That's kind of hard to do when she gained attention from four well-known gangsters as well as several criminal wanna-be's who decided that going after her will keep the gangsters in line. They don't know who they're dealing with nor does Melise as she learns the capabilities of the Marquis brothers and their determination to make her their woman.

She is resistant, has a lot on her plate, isn't quite willing to take a chance even though being with them makes her feel protected and important. She wants love, and a commitment, but everything about these men labels them players, and in all honesty, the emotions, attraction, and lust is mutual, and taking a chance on them as they take a chance on her, changes their destinies.

Genres: Contemporary, Ménage a Trois/Quatre, Romantic Suspense

Length: 35,789

HEALING HEARTS 17: TAKING CHANCES

Dixie Lynn Dwyer

Siren Publishing, Inc.
www.SirenPublishing.com

A SIREN PUBLISHING BOOK

Healing Hearts 17: Taking Chances
Copyright © 2019 by Dixie Lynn Dwyer

ISBN: 978-1-64243-749-2
First Publication: February 2019
Cover design by Les Byerley
All art and logo copyright © 2019 by Siren Publishing, Inc.

PUBLISHER
Siren Publishing, Inc.
www.SirenPublishing.com

ABOUT THE AUTHOR

People seem to be more interested in my name than where I get my ideas for my stories from. So I might as well share the story behind my name with all my readers.

My momma was born and raised in New Orleans. At the age of twenty, she met and fell in love with an Irishman named Patrick Riley Dwyer. Needless to say, the family was a bit taken aback by this as they hoped she would marry a family friend. It was a modern day arranged marriage kind of thing and my momma downright refused.

Being that my momma's families were descendants of the original English speaking Southerners, they wanted the family blood line to stay pure. They were wealthy and my father's family was poor.

Despite attempts by my grandpapa to make Patrick leave and destroy the love between them, my parents married. They recently celebrated their sixtieth wedding anniversary.

I am one of six children born to Patrick and Lynn Dwyer. I am a combination of both Irish and a true Southern belle. With a name like Dixie Lynn Dwyer it's no wonder why people are curious about my name.

Just as my parents had a love story of their own, I grew up intrigued by the lifestyles of others. My imagination as well as my need to stray from the straight and narrow made me into the woman I am today.

For all titles by Dixie Lynn Dwyer, please visit
www.bookstrand.com/dixie-lynn-dwyer

HEALING HEARTS 17: TAKING CHANCES

DIXIE LYNN DWYER
Copyright © 2019

Prologue

Melise Minter sat in the meeting because her boss, Eleanor, was sick. She wasn't happy about this, nor at the way the four bosses gazed at her body and tried to smile and over-welcome her to the meeting, which obviously pissed off Camille Spay. Office slut. The blonde bimbo wore way too much makeup and so much perfume that it was choking Melise out. Kelly, who worked in Internet promotions department, swore that Camille sprayed herself with perfume after she had sex with one of the bosses in their offices. Melise couldn't get that thought out of her head. It nauseated her, especially seeing how Camille always took credit for work she didn't do and completely slacked in her department. There was no way Camille could take credit for anything Melise did, because that took training, a Master's degree in computer design, and an ability to use a specialized program that was another six months of training to complete.

The problem she ran into searching for jobs was that there weren't many nearby, and she couldn't commute too far in case her brother or parents needed her. She tried not to focus on that or her brother's illness. His PTSD seemed to be getting worse, and she needed to find him some additional help. Her other brothers, Ben and Phoenix, were adamant about it because they were soldiers, as well, and didn't want to admit to the vulnerability and weakness they felt having their brother suffering from PTSD. She got that. They were having his back, keeping him strong, but ultimately not seeking help was going to make matters worse, not better.

"In about ten minutes, Masterson Reynolds, a very wealthy businessman, will be joining us to discuss his company and the product he wants to promote, and we must all be on board to appease him. He's hard to deal with, demanding, a perfectionist, and whatever he wants, we have to accommodate any way we can. This project has the potential to be in the millions. I want this deal. I want a contract with them that could last years if done correctly. Please be on the top of your game right now," William Wayworth said to them.

Melise sat there quietly as they discussed a few things about the company. This Masterson Reynolds had created a line of products for men. Everything from shaving cream and organic soaps, to aftershave, and now he was getting into a clothing line. It peaked Melise's interest.

When someone buzzed in that he was there, Camille looked ready to jump out of her seat. She fixed her lipstick, adjusted her top, the wench. Melise sighed and, sure enough, as her bosses stood up to greet the man who entered the room with two other men, Melise gulped. The guy was good-looking and then some. Dark grey shirt, linen, dress pants, stylish black designer shoes matching, he reeked of sophistication and wealth in a casual manner. His two sidekicks—big, definitely security, but they seemed to play it off as being consultants— eyed everyone in the room with accusation and distrust. She could feel it, and it made her belly quiver slightly. She was used to men and women in powerful positions of wealth and confidence. It came with the business, and as long as she didn't have to deal with them head on, she was fine. Luckily, in her position, she was behind the scenes, taking information, pictures, and ideas and bringing them to life in everything from print ads to commercials, to mini Internet ads. Enough to snag attention, peak people's interest, and link them to the product she was presenting.

Mr. Reynolds scanned the room with his two buddies as Mr. Wayworth began introductions. Mr. Reynolds gazed over Melise's body as Camille placed her hand on his arm and flirted. "Such a pleasure seeing you again. Please, have a seat right here next to me.

That way if you have any questions I can be sure to assist you," she said to him, but Mr. Reynolds looked at Melise.

"And you are?" he asked.

Melise opened her mouth to speak when Camille cut her off with a dismissive wave of her hand. "She isn't important. Just sitting in for her boss, Eleanor, who is out today."

"Melise is in charge of computer imaging and designs. A different department than marketing and promotions, but she will more than likely be pulled into the project along the way," Mr. Wayworth said and smiled at Melise. She swore the man licked his lips, and she felt annoyed, however, Mr. Reynolds reached his hand out to shake hers, bumping Camille in the process, which made Melise give Mr. Reynolds an even bigger smile in greeting.

The way the man stared at her, holding her gaze with those dark blue eyes of his, caught her off guard. She had to look away, and when she did, she locked gazes with one of his associates that he didn't introduce anyone to. Odd.

"Shall we begin?" Camille asked, and Melise took a seat as the others joined them.

It was a pretty interesting meeting, aside from Camille's annoying flirtatious remarks and airhead laughter at inappropriate times. Melise ignored her and jotted down some ideas if the company was to get this contract and move forward with a promotional campaign. Some folders were passed around containing all the products, as well as the new line of clothing by Mr. Reynolds. Melise could imagine the male models, all debonair, sexy, sporting the fine lined button-down shirts, the designer dress pants, or even shorts as they leaned against a Lamborghini and batted sensual eyes at the camera.

As Camille started to talk about how she saw the advertising going, Melise glanced up and locked gazes with the one man who sat beside Mr. Reynolds, and he was watching her. She gave a soft smile but one that pursed her lips, before she looked away.

"We can get things started for you with some ideas from marketing. Perhaps a shoot overseas? Paris, Italy, or even London might do," Camille said and batted her eyes at Mr. Reynolds.

"I'm a very busy man, plus the designs I've come up with were created in this area, not out of the country," he told her, and she nodded.

"Well, we could make due with something around here, I suppose," Camille said and tapped the pen to her bottom lip.

"Melise, you've come up with some amazing placements to portray the right mode for other products. Where do you see us setting up a shoot and getting some nice shots?" Mr. Wayworth asked her, and she wasn't too surprised. The man did love her work, but he never pulled her out of a crowd to ask a question. He must really want this contract, because she'd turned down his offers of dinner several times over the past year.

"She doesn't know. Eleanor will be back in tomorrow and will have some ideas. She and I will work on a setting. Melise just takes the final photos and then comes up with the commercial, magazine, and Internet ads," Camille said with an attitude. The woman hadn't a clue how much Melise did for this company.

"Actually, I do a lot more than that. However, my skills do lie in the actual designing of your promotional, commercial, and Internet ads, as well as helping to grab potential customers' attention and make them check out your brand. It's all how you perceive your product to be received, and who you believe your audience to be, Mr. Reynolds."

Mr. Reynolds squinted at her as he leaned back in his seat. He glanced at the other man, who had yet to take his eyes off of her. The other man nodded toward her, interrupting Camille and some nonsense about totally having an understanding for the audience and being able to bring that out with the marketing department. Everyone knew that the woman was clueless and stole other people's ideas.

"You were jotting down things in your notebook. What was that about?" the other man asked, his English accent thick. She felt her cheeks warm.

"Just some notes," she replied.

"Melise, if you have some ideas, some creative aspect to this, please share them. Mr. Reynolds and his associates are very important clients, and I promised them we would do whatever they asked to ensure success here," Mr. LaGrange, one of her other bosses, said to her.

"Well, as you were describing your clothing line and then after looking briefly at the pictures, just a few ideas, well, images danced in my head," she began to explain.

"Like?" he pushed.

"Like a male model wearing one of the pastel-colored linen dress shirts, partially unbuttoned, the designer dress pants in a light beige, hand in one pocket and the other, I don't know, perhaps running through his hair, showing a very expensive, platinum designer watch. He's leaning against a fancy car, like a Lamborghini or something eye-catching. He's near the beach, the sun is setting behind him, and there's the ad in a magazine, a commercial, or wherever with a bottle of your fragrance, the beach scent, light, shower fresh, I assume."

He smiled softly and leaned forward, but Masterson Reynolds just stared at her. "And is this model wearing shoes?" he asked, and Camille snickered, but Melise was quick on her toes.

"No, his shoes, a tan designer pair by Mr. Reynolds, are sitting on the car, and in another ad he could be facing the water. A beautiful woman, also shoeless," she winked, "could be making her way into his arms, her heels in her hand, her back foot lifted as he pulls her close. She inhales against his neck, loving the smell of him and that glorious cologne," she said, eyes closed, inhaling and then exhaling. She totally could see it. When she opened her eyes, her bosses all looked excited, and the three men stared at her, their expressions unreadable. Perhaps they didn't like her ideas. Oh well, not her concern. She looked down at her notepad until the nameless man spoke.

"You approve, Cader?" Mr. Reynolds asked.

The man, Cader, looked at Mr. Reynolds. "My interest is peaked," he replied.

"Very good. Let's get the ball rolling," Mr. Reynolds said, and Mr. Wayworth and the other bosses smiled ear to ear, but Camille gave Melise the evil eye.

Melise waited as the meeting came to an end. She shook their hands good-bye and then shook Mr. Wayworth's hand. He didn't release it but pulled her to the side as Camille accompanied Mr. Reynolds and his associates—Cader, and she believed Cader called the other man Sal—out of the meeting room. She overhead Camille saying something about lunch, but the men declined.

"You were amazing, Melise. Absolutely amazing. The way you drew them in with your ideas, your eyes closed, as if you truly envisioned their products, the scene in your head. I loved it. I want to set you up with some meetings with their product manager. He can give you all the details on every product, that way you can help come up with something spectacular."

"I usually come up with something using the computer software program, and then transition the material to magazine ads, commercials, and so forth once Eleanor and Camille pull ideas from the clients."

"You got us this contract, Melise. He wants you right there helping to run things. Reynolds is a busy businessman, and this product line is his baby. I will keep you posted on what I need," he said and caressed her arms. She got a creepy feeling and stepped back.

"This isn't her job, it's mine. I had a plan in motion," Camille interrupted.

"Your plan wasn't received well, Camille. Sometimes thinking out of the box works best. You can still meet with Mr. Reynolds and his associates and run the marketing campaign, just be sure that Melise is on board so she can come up with more great ideas. Melise can fill you in and you can present those ideas, the ads, the commercial ideas to Mr. Reynolds. Now, I need to get moving. Great job, ladies," Mr. Wayworth said and then walked away.

She knew from office gossip that Camille would take credit for other people's hard work and ideas, and her boss just gave the okay for that. It made Melise's chest burn with annoyance for a moment. That was basically what she would do here with these men. Well, she wasn't about to let that happen. As she started to leave, Camille grabbed her arm and pulled her back. With clenched teeth and a red face, Camille gave her a little push with her finger.

"You listen here, Melise, you're a nobody. I run the show and I get the clients to continue to invest in this company, to trust this company with their businesses. Your little display grabbed the contract, so kudos to you for that, but from here on out, Mr. Reynolds and his two associates are mine. I will be the ones meeting with them, presenting our ideas to them."

"You mean my ideas to them, don't you?" Melise asked.

"My ideas, not yours. I can get you fired as quickly as they hired you."

"I don't think so. You see, what I do is specialized and required years of schooling and, on top of that, more years to be expert certified. You don't have my credentials."

"I have better than that. I have the bosses wrapped around my finger. I also can get rid of you by making you look bad, perhaps screwing up some big clients' accounts. I have access to things, to computers, to accounts, to information that could bring this entire company to the ground. So, don't mess with me. I expect some ideas, photos, descriptions, etcetera on my desk tomorrow end of day."

Melise felt her blood pressure rise. She was so annoyed at Camille, but she did hear that she had caused multiple people in Wayworth Industries to quit or get fired. She had access to things because she spread her legs for the bosses. She was a witch. Melise needed this job. She didn't want to lose it and wind up commuting an hour to work each day and an hour back. What if her parents or her brother needed her, then what? No, she could do this. More than likely, Mr. Wayworth would know they were Melise's ideas and not Camille's. She exhaled in annoyance. She was stuck having to deal with this crazy woman, but either way, she got paid, and money paid the bills.

Melise headed back to her office and straight to her computer. She put the meeting aside, not bothering to think about what would come next, how annoying Camille might be to her, or what the evil woman might pull. She would focus on the job and the paycheck. When her cell phone rang, and she glanced at the caller I.D. and felt the instant knot in her stomach. She picked it up quickly. "Hello?"

"Everything is okay," her mother said. "I just wanted to be sure that you were still coming over Saturday. He needs to see you. He's been asking about the painting."

She closed her eyes and thought about her brother, Elliott. For some strange reason, watching her paint as soft classical music played in the background calmed him down. Otherwise, he had episodes of violence, some verbal, some physical, and they didn't end well. Her other brothers, Phoenix and Ben, had to step in.

"I'll be there, Mom. I'll be there."

Chapter 1

"Jordan, come on, man, you got this." Pelham sat on the floor by his brother. He was having an episode. Though few and far between, Jordan still got caught up in the nightmares every now and then. The last several months they had used their capabilities to help rescue some of their friends' women who had gotten into trouble. Jordan had done a lot of recon for those rescues, and it weighed on him.

"I'll be fine. Just leave me."

"No, Jordan. I got your back. Carson and Warren, too. Come on, man," Pelham said.

"Just leave me the fuck alone. I got this. I'm not a fucking baby, a fucking nut job. I got it. Go!" he yelled at them.

Pelham stood up. "We're staying right here."

They took position in the bedroom. Pelham on the floor at the end of the bed, Carson in the hallway by the door, and Warren in the recliner in the corner. They would never leave their brother's side during an episode. For a year, he tried to hide them from his brothers, but some were pretty damn bad. It took some counseling, someone they could trust, but it helped. Pelham was concerned today because they had a job to do, some investigating into a guy who was now working for a businessman they all knew. Since they took over ownership of the boatyard and marina, as well as the storefronts in Fulton with Costanza, Merdock, and Covaney, they ran into a bit of trouble. Some investors were looking to buy up properties in the vicinity and were also attempting to muscle their property manager, Enrique Sotos. Pelham, his brothers, and the Lopez brothers were trying to keep their ownership on the down low, but with exposure like they had now, it was hard. Whoever these men were trying to push a sale hadn't a clue who they were dealing with. Before doing anything rash, Pelham, Carson, Warren, and Jordan needed to look into the men and their agenda.

Pelham's phone rang just as Jordan eased his head back.

"I'm good. I'm fine," Jordan whispered, and then started to get up and just like that, it passed. The worry in the pit of Pelham's gut eased knowing Jordan pulled through once again. Those episodes, his fits of rage, holding him down, begging him to bring his mind back to the present seemed gone forever. Then he had little ones like this one out of the blue. He narrowed his eyes and gave Warren and Carson a nod to stay with Jordan as he answered the call.

"Pelham."

"Caught wind of a business transaction in Trenton. Thinking you may be interested in knowing about it," Eduardo Cruz said to him.

"Go ahead," Pelham replied.

"Merser Volcheck and Dolinth Ferchosky bought out Simon and that storefront of upscale stores on Avenue West."

"I didn't know it was up for sale."

"No one did. Merser had the inside information on it, but, interesting enough, the place has a storage facility on site, and guess what's being imported in and out to Florida and the U.S. Virgin Islands?"

"Drugs."

"And guns, and stolen merchandise from the Northeast. It's a holding facility."

"So, that's why Merser bought that estate on the bay and has been hosting so many events. He's playing up a legit side of business in the fashion industry. Wonder if he's also loading up hot designer merchandise."

"You got it."

"Could make for some profit on our end, considering they'd want to ensure security and pay the fee for setting up shop in Lopez territory."

"Exactly. Keep in mind, Merser contacted me about some rare art he came into, through a friend, of course."

"Of course."

"I'm game if it's not that hot," Eduardo replied.

"Watch your ass with him, but I appreciate the information. I'll pass it along and take action as necessary and instructed."

"Great. Talk to you soon."

Pelham ended the call. He would need to discuss things with Costanza. See how he wanted to approach a confrontation. Their jobs lay in various areas—everything from business opportunities and investments as entrepreneurs, to providing muscle to lay on the push to get what was needed. They had connections and capabilities from various areas and could choke out information on people when necessary. He didn't know if this situation would lead to anything more than getting money to protect Merser and Dolinth's business venture. They chose an area under multiple families' control, so they must be willing to pay, which means their profits were outstanding.

"What's going on?" Carson asked, coming into the living room with his brothers in tow. One look at Jordan and he knew his brother was in a mood. It would be better to not send him on intel to get answers. He could kill someone instead of just scaring the shit out of them.

"Eduardo has some information on a new business investment of Merser and Dolinth's. They're setting up shop in Trenton. Technically, Lopez territory. Bringing in drugs, guns, stolen designer merchandise, and art."

"Costanza is going to be pissed off that he wasn't made aware of this," Warren said to him.

"I need to confirm with him first," Pelham replied.

"Whatever you need, I'm in," Jordan said, fists flexing by his sides. A ticking time bomb.

"Not necessary right now. I don't want to jump the gun. There's money to be made from this, and we'll ensure we get our cut just like Costanza and his brothers will. Let me talk to him, and then we'll head out."

"I'm not going to dinner. I got something else to do," Jordan said and then walked out of the room.

* * * *

The classical music played in the background, a melody by Chopin, one of Elliott's favorites. Melise relaxed her mind, knowing he could sense her emotions. They were close. Only fourteen months apart in age, practically twins. As she painted and he watched her work on the canvas, a landscape of the house on the ocean, kids playing on the beach, the parents nearby. It reminded them all of when they were younger and did such activities. He sat in a chair by the porch alongside her, and her mom cooked in the kitchen, the smell of pies baking from earlier now turned into aromas of roasted chicken in the oven. The aroma inspired more memories of growing up, their mom's cooking a staple to the family bond they shared.

Before long, it was time to stop. Dinner was ready. Elliott lay sleeping on the couch looking calm, peaceful, and instead of a smile it brought tears to her eyes. He was so strong, so capable, and the PTSD, the nightmares weakened him too much. She wanted to talk to him about a program she learned about through her friend Kai. There was a therapist, Kiana, who had helped a lot of soldiers and civilians with their PTSD. Melise had spoken to her several times, and she was willing to meet Elliott.

As soon as she moved, her brother awoke with a start, sat forward, eyes bloodshot, looking exhausted. Her heart ached for him.

"Rest, Elliott," she said softly.

He rubbed his eyes and then cleared his throat. "How long was I out?" he asked, and she could see the hope in his eyes. That the number she told him would somehow ease his mind and help him in some way. But it wasn't that long.

"Maybe twenty minutes." The disappointment and anger covered his face. She got up and went to him. "I met someone I would like you to meet. To talk to."

"No. No therapists and that bullshit. I got this," he snapped at her.

She took his hand. "Elliott, she's really nice and she's worked with so many people. Civilians and soldiers. She gets it."

"No. This helps me. Being here with family helps."

"But what about at the house with Ben and Phoenix? Things can get better, easier with the right coping mechanisms, the right therapy and techniques to calm your mind and help you get back that control you need and deserve."

He shook his head and stood up. She stepped back.

"Let's have dinner." He then glanced at the painting. Their mom entered the room.

"Turn off the music. It's annoying," he snapped, and Melise knew he was done. The relaxing time, the time he grabbed onto, was over.

Chapter 2

"You've been working like a dog, what's the newest campaign?" Nina asked Melise as Sue grabbed them another round of mimosas, and Antonia flipped onto her belly. They were all sunbathing in the backyard by the pool at the Lopez brothers' estate.

"It's been hell. Not the campaign as much as it's Camille. She is so nasty, and basically, she's been taking my ideas and Eleanor's and presenting them to the clients. The bosses are thrilled, so not much I can do."

"That's ridiculous. They have to know that they're your ideas," Antonia said to her.

"They do, I'm sure of it, and it isn't like I would get paid more for presenting the ideas, it's just knowing that witch is right there taking credit. She threatened me on day one, telling me about her access to programs, the computer systems, and how she could pretty much sabotage me to make me look bad."

"Jesus, you should find a different job to work at. Your credentials and skills are specialized, so why not?" Nina asked.

"I can't do a farther commute. I have personal obligations with my family, and if there was an emergency, then I wouldn't be able to get to them quick enough," she said to them.

"What's the campaign, and how long will this particular project take?" Sue asked.

Melise took a sip of her mimosa. "Men's clothing and fragrances, very classy and yet everyday wear. The cologne is to die for. It smells so good."

"Really? Anything I would want to get for my men?" Nina asked and smiled.

"I could probably get samples. I'm supposed to check out the shoot where they'll be doing the commercial. My ideas, of course, that Camille claimed as her own, however, she can't do what I do with the computer designs and software. I can make serious changes, bring it to life, and add a sexy allure to it. I have everything set to go ahead of schedule, but now I have to go to the shoot."

"That has to be a lot of fun though. It does sound like you're enthusiastic about the products," Francesca told her.

"Oh, I am, it's just the nonsense with Camille around. I swear she's trying to seduce the owner of the company and his buddies just to be sure to claim she made the deal happen. It's disgusting and also sophomoric. I wish I could find something more professional and with people who actually support one another in the workforce and aren't out to spread their legs to gain kudos," Melise replied.

"Who is spreading their legs for kudos?" Cobra asked, coming onto the patio with Costanza, Eduardo Cruz, and Pelham Marquis. Melise's gaze went right to Pelham, and she couldn't tell where he was looking because of the dark sunglasses he wore. Eduardo, however, was in a dead stare at Francesca, who lay her head back down onto the lounge chair as she lay on her belly.

Melise felt her belly quiver and her heart race. Whenever she saw Pelham, Carson, and Warren she felt an attraction to them, and they flirted a little but not too much. She found out from Francesca that they were in the military at one time. That Warren and Pelham got out earlier, then Carson and another brother, whom no one ever saw, got out soon after.

"Just that office slut Melise is forced to work with. So, are you guys all done with your meeting?" Nina asked. Costanza walked over to her, placed his finger under her chin, and she tilted up toward him to touch her lips to his.

"We sure are, and ready to relax by the pool and enjoy a dinner with friends," Merdock said, joining them with the other men. Melise closed her eyes and lay out in the sun while Nina's men showed the others to the cabana and the outdoor bar.

"I didn't know they were going to be here," Melise said to Antonia.

Antonia bit her lower lip. "I didn't either. I swear Eduardo makes me so nervous. He's like a mob boss or something."

"I know what you mean," Melise added and raised both her eyebrows, then exhaled.

"Pelham, Carson, and Warren? Seriously? Are you out of your mind?" Antonia asked.

"Me? No, I haven't initiated or responded to anything Pelham and his brothers have said to me."

"Yet. Eduardo intimidates me big time. I think we're both in some serious trouble here."

"Not if we leave. I can send you a text and you can send me one?" Melise suggested.

"Chicken?" Melise asked.

"Look at them and you tell me," Antonia chuckled.

"We're in this together, let's just remain close. Nothing can happen with friends nearby."

Melise wasn't sure about that at all.

* * * *

"See something you like?" Vin asked Pelham as they got cold beers from the tiki bar.

"What do you mean?" Pelham asked, and took a slug from the bottle of Stella.

"Come on, man, you and your brothers have had your eyes on Melise for months now. Why aren't you making a move?"

"Hey, don't go trying to play matchmaker. You know we deal with heavy shit. Don't need to worry about a woman or the potential problems that come with one."

"Yeah right. I can tell you from experience that nothing else will matter if there's an attraction there. By the way you stopped short and stared at the woman's body, I think it's safe to say you're attracted to her."

"Who the fuck wouldn't be? She looks like a model, has an incredible body, and is very professional."

"All great qualities for men of your standards and capabilities."

Pelham tore his eyes away from Melise for a moment and looked at Vin. "Can't do it to Jordan. It wouldn't be fair or right."

Vin squinted. "He's still having issues?"

"Not as frequently, and he isn't here with us, so what does that tell you?" Pelham asked.

"Well, I guess all you can do is keep being there for him and help him to get stronger. You shouldn't not pursue an interest, though. I can tell you first hand, stubbornness and excuses can only hold you back for so long."

Pelham looked back toward Melise.

"She's single," Vin added and chuckled. "What? Enjoy yourselves, like Eduardo is doing right now with Antonia."

"The woman looks scared."

"She should be. Eduardo is powerful and suave with the ladies. Antonia seems old school."

"Like Melise."

A few minutes later as Pelham noticed Melise joining the conversation between Eduardo and Antonia, he walked over and joined them. The woman was stunning. She had long brown hair, bright green eyes, and full, soft lips. Her body was perfect, and her skin tan and wet from perspiration. It was pretty damn hot out.

"Need a drink?" he asked her. She looked up toward him, her lips parted, and she shook her head. "You look like you do," he told her, gazing over those sexy curves, her full breasts pushed together by the bikini top that deepened her cleavage.

"I think a dip in the pool will help," Antonia said and started to get up from the lounge chair. Eduardo took her hand and helped her up. Pelham did the same for Melise, and he pulled a little too much and their bodies collided.

"Oh God, so sorry," she said to him.

He took the opportunity to graze her lower back and hip with his hand before releasing her. "No problem at all. I'll join you," he said as he stepped back and pulled off his shirt. He had already changed into swim trunks. He caught her gaze over his body, and he knew he looked good. He and his brothers trained like crazy, always ready to defend themselves or counterattack whether they were in casual attire or suits. Most of their jobs in the past were as heavies—men putting pressure on people needed to comply for their bosses' businesses. They'd come a long way from being the bodyguards. Now, they were the heavies, bosses themselves. The ones with power to assist those in need, and they gained a respect in the families and in the business circuit so everyone knew to not fuck with them or their friends.

He watched Melise slowly step into the water after Antonia and Eduardo went in. Carson and Warren were in the pool already and talking to Nolte, Cane, Merdock, and Covaney, while Costanza and Vin remained by the outdoor bar. His brothers looked toward Melise as she swam in the water to cool off. The pool had built-in seats along the sides made to enjoy drinks by the pool and still be in the water. Costanza and Vin handed out some more cold beers and then some kind of mixed drinks for the ladies. Warren took one for Melise and offered her a seat along the side next to him and Carson. She took it as she sat on the edge of the pool, the water dripping along her breast and her belly, then against the tiny gold belly ring he almost missed.

"Haven't seen you in a while, Melise, what have you been up to?" Carson asked her, taking a slug from his beer, holding her gaze.

"Just working a lot," she replied, shy like usual. He was pretty sure they intimidated her.

Warren looked her over. "You look amazing. Still doing those kickboxing classes at Donny York's dojo?"

She looked surprised. "How did you know that?"

"I was in there one day visiting him for a favor he needed and I caught sight of you going into the class."

She nodded. "I do still go but to the five a.m. class now."

"That's early," Carson said to her.

She looked at him. "Not enough hours in the day. I have to go early, or by the time I get home from work I start making excuses, so it ensures I get it done."

"Good for you."

"How about you guys, do you work out there?"

"No, we have our own gym and set up at the house. Got everything we need and one another to beat up on," Warren said, smirking.

"Who beats up on whom? I'm pretty sure I always wind up last man standing," Pelham teased.

"Bullshit, last man standing. Usually it's Jordan," Warren said and chuckled. Pelham felt his gut clench. He didn't want to bring up Jordan or worry about the guilt he felt having some fun, flirting with Melise and knowing he couldn't take it further.

"Who's Jordan?" she asked and took a sip from her drink.

"Our brother," Carson said, straight-faced.

"You guys have another brother? So, there's four of you?" she asked.

"Doesn't matter," Pelham snapped and gave Carson and Warren mean looks.

Melise slid down from the seat. "Well, I need to dry off, then help with the food." She walked out of the pool, and they watched her.

"What the fuck?" Warren whispered to him.

Pelham gave him a dirty look. "You don't bring up Jordan. Not ever. It isn't right or fair."

"Pelham, she's gorgeous, sexy, and sweet, and we're all attracted to her. What's the big fucking deal?" Warren asked.

"We can't make any kind of commitment. Jordan needs us to be there for him. A woman could get in the way, unless you're talking about something temporary."

"Really, Pelham? Even I can tell she isn't a temporary person. Hell, I was going to ask her out, but then you ruined that shit by basically barking at her."

"I didn't bark."

"You sure the fuck did," Carson now added, too.

"Whatever. Do whatever the fuck you want."

* * * *

Warren was a bit annoyed at Pelham, but he knew where he was coming from. None of them wanted to make Jordan feel left out or not good enough, and sometimes it was extra difficult. Like right now, when the three of them were attracted to a woman, wanted to get to know her better and see where it led, and they couldn't do that. Couldn't pursue a woman, except for sex and nothing more. Certainly, they couldn't go after a woman like Melise. She would expect commitment, a steady relationship, and none of them ever did that. Perhaps Pelham was right to stop the conversation from continuing and make Melise see them for who they really were. Hardcore, shrewd businessmen, who didn't date women but screwed them.

* * * *

Melise grabbed her painting materials and headed to the pier in Mercy. She had a few hours left until sunset, and she wanted to put the week behind her, including the odd conversation with those Marquis brothers last weekend at the Lopez estate. What a nasty jerk Pelham was. After all, he approached her first, engaged her with his brothers. Obviously, they were after a little action. Typical. She pushed thoughts of them aside and set up her easel and the canvas. She didn't have time for games, for dating, or even just sex. It wasn't what she wanted, what she knew she needed in life. A life that had become monotonous. She closed up her heart to caring for anyone else other than her brothers and her parents, and, of course, her friends. Men? Too much aggravation trying to figure out their games and tactics that were ultimately for sex.

She took a seat and looked across the water at the beach down below and the people gathering up their belongings or setting up some cocktails to enjoy the sunset. With each stroke, she got lost in the scene, allowing her mind to be free and thoughts to scatter about around work, pleasure, and the envious feeling she currently had. A couple on the beach set up their chairs and a small table and began to open wine, share a glass along with some cheese and crackers, maybe. She couldn't make it out from here, but the wine was obvious, and so was the attraction. They shared a kiss, and she continued to paint.

She didn't even mind the people passing by enjoying her work, since she ignored them and continued to paint, the scene so vivid—the multi-colored sky as the sun began to slowly move, the flowing water, the shimmering beach, all captured on canvas as she worked as quickly as she could. She sensed someone behind her now. Not too close, but they were there for a while. She didn't mind, and they weren't hovering. As the sun got lower and lower, she leaned back and looked from the view that was now, to what she captured on canvas.

"Amazing," the male voice whispered, so deep and effective. She turned to look way up and saw a very tall man, and he was gorgeous. He had scruff along his cheeks, green eyes, she thought, and muscles galore protruding from a military t-shirt.

"Thanks," she whispered and then pushed a loose strand of hair behind her ear. She stood up, and he just stared at the picture, emotion filling his eyes, making them sparkle instead of looking dull like a few seconds ago.

"How do you do it?" he asked her, then glazed over her body. She felt it. Holy hell did she feel it.

She stuttered, "I don't know. I just do it. Just paint what I see, what I feel."

"It's incredible. I've watched you here before and was impressed with your pieces, and this, this captured a moment now lost to anyone else who hadn't had the chance to view it live," he told her, and she looked back at the painting and then at the darker rays of colors, the sun long gone and the shadows of light lingering a little longer across the beach.

She felt a little uneasy that he said he had watched her before. He looked rugged, and he was unshaven, hair disheveled. She saw the tattoos on his arms, the marine symbol, and gulped, then started to pack up her things.

"What do you do with them when you finish? Are they on display in a gallery or something?"

"Oh God, no, they're just for me, or maybe family. I have a bunch. It helps me to relax and to let go of the stresses of life, I guess."

"That's a shame. I mean, everyone should get to enjoy this and appreciate your work."

"Thanks."

"I mean it, really. I've seen others painting, and they don't come to life. This one relaxes me," he said to her. When there was suddenly a large bang, a garbage truck or something dropping the metal garbage bin right across the way, the man jumped, turned ready for action, and her heart raced. He didn't move, focused on what was happening, and then straightened out. He looked around them, seemed unsure, and she recognized his reaction, his stance. He had PTSD.

"It's okay," she said and placed her hand over her heart. He narrowed his eyes at her, and she continued, "My heart is racing. So silly of me to have gotten scared like that." It seemed to make him feel less embarrassed maybe, or think she didn't notice his reaction too much.

"Are you leaving right now?" he asked, and something told her he really wanted to keep looking at the painting. She thought about her brother, Elliott. How strong he was, filled with muscles, capable, and yet became so vulnerable and weak at the simplest things.

"I have some time. I'm trying to decide where I'll sit next time. When I'll have the time to come back."

"You work besides painting?"

"Yes, for a marketing company in Trenton."

"Designing ads, I bet," he said and gave a soft smile again, looking her over. She didn't even look good, wearing a pair of cotton black shorts, a tank top, and tennis sneakers. He towered over her, too, and with looks like his, he could be swarmed with women. As she stared into his eyes, it was like she knew him or recognized him, and she squinted.

"I'm not some creep or something. Just curious about my magic painter," he said and stepped closer to the painting.

"Your magic painter?" she asked him.

He glanced at her. "That's the nickname I gave you weeks ago when I first saw you around the pier."

She snickered. "Nice."

"Well, I'm glad I met you…" He waited for her to say her name.

"Melise."

"Melise? Beautiful name. I'm Jordan." He reached his hand out for her to shake and when she did, she was shocked at the instant connection she felt. His eyes widened and then squinted. Then he looked back at the painting, and she could tell he was calmer now than a few minutes earlier.

As she gathered her things, she watched him and didn't think twice. "Why don't you keep it, Jordan?"

He swung his head up to look at her. "What?"

"The painting is yours to keep."

"No, I couldn't do that. You said you don't sell them or display them."

"I don't, but I know when someone really appreciates the artwork and it touches them, like it touched me. I think that's more important than any monetary value, or to do like I do with the others and just wrap them up and store them."

"That's insane. Are you sure?"

"I'm certain," she said, and he stared at her.

"You'll sign it?" he asked.

"You want me to?"

"You'll be famous one day when you let go of those stored paintings and begin to sell them," he told her and winked. She chuckled and then grabbed her brush and some black paint and signed it for him with the date.

"Can I at least buy you dinner?" he asked.

"That isn't necessary, and I don't really know you."

"You gave me a painting you spent several hours on, you can't trust me to buy you dinner?" he asked, tilting his head just so and looking so damn attractive.

"Something simple."

"Taco place on the corner?" he asked.

"Love that place."

"Good. Let's go." He held the painting and she carried her things, and they walked together along the pier until they got to the taco shop. She ordered the taco salad, and he ordered some tacos. They talked, and she found him mysterious in a lot of ways. He didn't share much, was not giving any details as he described his work, something in business and securities. His phone kept going off, and he was getting annoyed.

"You can answer those if it's important. Seems to be," she said to him.

He exhaled then pulled out his cell phone, texted angrily on it, and then pressed send.

"Girlfriend?" she asked. He squinted at her, and she felt stupid for saying that. The thought actually made her feel jealous and stupid. She didn't know this guy. She didn't date, plus she was bad at picking the right men. Look at how she was attracted to Pelham, Carson, and Warren and how rude they were. She was so attracted to them she didn't even mind that they were made men, into criminal activities and carried guns.

"No girlfriend. Haven't had one actually in years."

"Years?" she asked, surprised, and took a sip of her water.

"Why do you say it like that?" he asked on the defensive.

She scrunched her eyes together. "You're very attractive and have that whole macho attitude, yet you flirt well and you're easy to talk to, that's all," she said and looked away.

"You shouldn't find me attractive. I have a bad side to me," he said, and when she glanced back toward him, he looked away. She didn't know why she was analyzing him so much, why he seemed readable, or why she assumed he was like her brother and suffered because of PTSD. It wasn't like she could tell him she got it, that she understood.

"A bad side, huh? Well then, I guess it was a smart move on my part to give you my painting. Now, I'm on your good side so you won't go all serial killer on me, right?" she asked.

He narrowed his eyes at her, an almost-smirk on his lips. "Serial killer? That isn't what I mean by bad side."

"Oh, whoops. Sometimes my creative energy goes to my brain. So, you mean you're a criminal, then?" she asked, and then took another bite of her salad. He snorted.

"I talked you into having dinner with me. We just met," he said to her and leaned forward in his chair and held her gaze all serious-like. "I could get you to give me your number. I could find out where you live. I could rob your place when you're at work, and you would never suspect me, because I would remain friendly like this, pretending to be nice when really I'm not."

She thought about this a moment. The conversation sure did change, and he got dark, like he was resisting something. She had him smiling slightly. Was he feeling vulnerable?

"So, you're pretending to be nice and ultimately you want to commit a crime against me, even though I gave you a piece of my heart, my creativity?" she asked holding his gaze.

He swallowed and just stared at her. "Where did you come from? Why aren't you scared of me? I said I have a dark side. Can't you see I..." He looked away.

"I get it," she said. She wiped her mouth and then took another sip of her iced tea.

"No, you don't, Melise."

"I do, Jordan. You've never met someone who was nice to you, who did something for you or gave you something without wanting something in return, and you can't process it or handle it, because of that dark side. No problem. It was nice meeting you. Enjoy that painting," she said and stood up. He reached out so quickly she gasped.

"Sit, please. Don't go, just sit here with me," he said to her, shocking her. She didn't know if she should or not, but the decision was made as she sat back down and held his gaze. The feel of his large hand encasing her small wrist like it was nothing made her feel way intimidated. If he were a killer, she would be dead in a flash. As if sensing her fear going up a notch, he released her wrist. "I'm sorry. I don't know how to act. How to flirt or talk to a woman like you."

"You were doing fine until the whole dark side thing," she said to him, and again he snickered and shook his head. He ran his fingers through his hair. He needed a haircut, yet it made him look sexy and untamed.

"You're not like most women," he said, holding her gaze.

"Oh boy, are we reaching for the lines now, because I've heard them all," she said, leaning back in her chair.

"No line, you aren't. It's so weird to be able to just talk to someone and not feel like I'm on eggshells or getting analyzed."

She swallowed hard. She was analyzing him in her mind. She felt badly. Maybe he was just a really nice guy. "I know what you mean. Why can't people just speak their minds? Oh wait, you did with the whole dark side thing."

"Okay, so maybe I was trying to put up a wall."

"I get that, too, and you know, we did just meet. I'm not exactly going to share any secrets with you or give you my number or tell you where I live."

"No number, seriously? But I thought I explained the dark side thing."

She chuckled. "Still worried about the whole potential serial killer or, at minimum, robber. I should warn you that I don't have much worth stealing at my place."

"You work in marketing, I find that difficult to believe."

"It's true. I don't like clutter."

"Then what do you do with all of those paintings?"

"Store them at a special place, a little studio I go to when the weather isn't nice."

"Around here?" he asked.

"Hmmm, not sharing anything personal," she teased.

He inhaled deeply, a small grin on his face. "When will you be back here on the pier painting?" he asked her.

"Sunday maybe."

"Can we do dinner again, after I watch you create another beautiful painting?" he asked, but his voice sounded different. Hesitant.

"How long were you watching me tonight?" she asked.

"Over an hour. When others began to walk by and stop, I moved from the bench to get closer. I was stunned by your abilities." He stared into her eyes.

"You always hang out by the pier in the evenings?"

"It relaxes me, you know, the sound of the ocean waves, the peacefulness."

"I know what you mean. I come down here at night sometimes and just sit in the sand and let my mind just go blank and not think, just breathe."

"You shouldn't come out here alone at night."

"It's Mercy, the Chief of Police runs a safe town. There are always people watching."

"Not every second, and a woman so sweet and beautiful as you could get grabbed. Then what would you do? Don't come here alone at night," he reprimanded her. "Listen, I told you I'm into security and things. Well, I've seen some bad stuff on jobs, had to rescue some drunk woman before a group of guys got her into their truck. She didn't know what was going on. Another woman had something slipped into her drink."

Her eyes widened. "I know about those types of things. All too well," she said.

"Please Melise, promise me you won't come out here alone at night and sit on the beach by yourself."

"What if I bring a flashlight and a baseball bat?" she asked him.

He stared at her, looked at her breasts in the tank top, and then her face. "How about I give you my number and you call me, and I'll come watch over you?"

"Hmmm, all that just to try and get my number?" she asked.

He shook his head. "All that, to make sure that you're safe. You're too sweet, too trusting."

"Because I spoke to you, gave you a painting, and had tacos with you? Has the world turned into such an evil place?"

"The world is an evil place, Melise, and you need to be prepared so you won't become a victim. I'll worry if you don't heed to my warning."

She stared at him a moment. "Okay, Jordan, I accept your warning, but not your phone number, otherwise you'll think I'm easy."

He shook his head. "You aren't easy, you're just too nice," he said. She shrugged her shoulders as they sat there and talked a little more before he walked to her car and they parted ways.

"Maybe I'll see you Sunday, then?" he asked.

"You never know. Thanks again for the tacos."

"Thank you for the painting," he said.

She got into her car with her supplies and headed out of the parking lot. It had been the strangest chance meeting she ever had, but also the most effective. She liked him. She hoped he wasn't a bad person, and with that thought, the walls came back up and she worried about seeing him again, and now would debate all week about coming back here Sunday. She must be losing her mind.

* * * *

Jordan watched Melise's car pull out of the parking lot. The woman was incredible, gorgeous, sexy, sweet, and so out of his league it wasn't even funny. Even if he didn't have PTSD, she would be too good for him. Too good for his brothers. That thought made him look back at his cell phone. They panicked over him not being home. He didn't blame them, not after last week and that episode. It came out of nowhere. He shook his head and then walked to his truck. He felt different.

Was it because of Melise? He looked at the painting. Her painting that she signed. Something that she didn't seem to share with just anyone, or that was how she made it sound. Was it true? It made him feel good. Maybe she lied. Women lied. People lied, always looking to get something from you. He got a little aggressive with his mouth, didn't know why he blurted out about a dark side. Was he trying to warn her away from him so it would be easier to forget her?

As he drove the truck, he kept glancing at the painting. She was so talented yet didn't know it. He supposed that was typical. For a person to not see their talent. He exhaled. What were his talents? His abilities? Beating the shit out of someone who didn't comply? Fighting, weaponry that he didn't use much anymore because he was retired from the service? His brothers pulled him into the businesses they ventured into. Some aspects he was good at, others he just followed their lead. It was an easy life now, and it sucked that his nightmares made him not want to live at all. He looked back at the painting.

He thought about Melise. He wanted to see her again. Would she want to see him? Would she show up Sunday, and if she did, would it be to see him or to just paint? Maybe she was being nice and wanted a friend? He didn't look at her and think *friend*. His body reacted, and that shocked him, as well. She did it for him. She made him feel, and he wanted more of the feeling, when he should be running from it. What did he have to offer her, when he took things a day at a time, not knowing what tomorrow might bring, or where his head may be at? Or whether he could lose his mind and decide to end it all? He pushed those thoughts away. Those were mind games from a year ago, from a darker time and a darker place. He fought to live and was going to see what would happen next. All he had to hope for was thinking about what tomorrow might bring his way.

Chapter 3

"Carmichael's, you do know the place, correct?" Camille asked with an attitude. The snob. Of course Melise knew it, she just never ate there because it was overpriced.

"What?" Melise asked Mr. Wayworth with Camille standing right next to him.

"After the shoot today, you're to have dinner with Masterson Reynolds and his associates, as well as two representatives from the production department, Mel and Frank. You remember them?" Mr. Wayworth said to her.

"Yes, of course I do," she replied, now putting together the text she got at six this morning from Eleanor warning her to wear something classy and stylish for an outing. She had been giving her the heads up because many times when Melise worked on designs she dressed in dress pants and a blouse. They were going to Carmichael's, and it was fancy.

"You're to discuss your evaluation of the shoot today, the first run on the ideas you and Camille came up with together," Mr. Wayworth said, and gave Camille a wink, and she smugly smiled, the bitch.

"Why not just send Camille to dinner with them?" Melise asked.

"That's what I said, but apparently they want your feedback on some things. I wasn't a hundred percent sure of how the designing worked, really, so you need to fill them in."

"Oh, but they were both of our ideas," she said sarcastically. Camille ground her teeth.

"They would like to hear your professional opinion and an explanation of how things will go down. Cader will be at the shoot with you, so remain by his side and answer any questions he may have."

"How can I do that and make sure the commercial is going according to my ideas?"

"You can handle it fine. I have confidence in you. Remember, Melise, whatever they want, accommodate them and keep them happy," he said with a wink before he exited the room. Why did she feel like she was being set up here?

An hour later, she was arguing with the director about the way the commercial was supposed to be going. "Why are all these women surrounding him? Where are they coming from?" she asked.

"Camille thought it made it seem sexier to have multiple women approach him and appear more like a god," the assistant producer told her.

"Seriously? No. Absolutely not. I mean, that's ludicrous. This isn't some cheap perfume made for teenage men to get lucky. It's a mature, classy, and expensive perfume that is to be distinguished above all others, same as the clothing line. Look at this actor. He's gorgeous, but he isn't supposed to look like a gigolo," she exclaimed. She then looked at Cader, and he was smirking. "What?"

He narrowed his eyes at her, still grinning, and stood up from one of those director chairs. "How do you see this commercial?" he asked.

She looked at the assistant producer. "Camille said—"

"Camille isn't here," she interrupted. "How long have we worked together? Have I ever come up with something as tacky as that? No."

"No, you haven't, but Mr. Reynolds and his associates allowed Camille to handle things," the assistant producer told her.

She was so frustrated right now. This was going to be the shittiest commercial ever, and when it failed, it wouldn't be Camille's name on it, it would have Melise's name on it. She lightly slapped her palm to her forehead and began to pace.

"Melise," Cader said. He grabbed her shoulders and she looked way up at the man and into those blue eyes of his. "I think Masterson and Sal were right, and that Camille is very jealous of your skills and talent. These weren't your ideas, were they?" he asked, and she shook her head no.

"I'm so sorry, Cader. I know this seems very unprofessional, but I swear I'll fix it. Today the commercial will be produced and completed. No more changes will happen."

"Okay. Masterson and Sal should be here any minute, so let's get this together and see what you got," he said to her and gave her arms a squeeze.

"Thank you. It will work out great."

She walked back over to the assistant producer.

"Okay, so this is how it's going down." She started to explain things and then picked the model that would play the guy's girlfriend. As she arranged the setup, Masterson and Sal came in.

"What is this?" he asked, and she overheard him talking to Cader, and Cader explained about the set up earlier.

"Melise, what's going on?" Masterson asked, and she excused herself a minute but told the male model to stay by the car where he was.

"Hello Mr. Reynolds, I'm so sorry about the confusion, but I believe you'll be happy with my ideas."

"I thought we had your ideas already. The multiple women swarming the man because he smells so good," he said.

She felt her nostrils flare, saw him squint, and she exhaled. She closed her eyes and breathed. "Okay, that wasn't my idea. This is, and this will make the commercial amazing, not that other teenage nonsense."

"I'm confused," Sal said.

"I think we should trust Melise. After all, it was her work, her imagery that sold us on this company," Cader said.

"Please, sir, I promise, you will love it, and if you don't, then I'll take full responsibility either way."

He stared down at her. The man was pretty big and a bit older, maybe mid-forties if she had to guess. "Okay, let's see what you have."

She turned around, took a deep breath, and then pulled off the top light sweater she wore and placed it near her purse. The slim fitting black dress hugged her body tight, and the V neckline revealed her deep cleavage. She wore several strands of necklaces and high heels to match but kicked them off so she could walk on the sand. She wanted to make sure she looked really good, and by the way the producer whistled at her and the model flirted, she'd say she pulled it off.

* * * *

"She is something else. You were right about Camille, just after our money, the bitch, and her ideas were terrible," Cader said to Masterson.

"I don't know, I kind of liked all those sexy women coming after the guy because of his clothes and perfume," Sal said.

"It isn't the look we're going for. We want to make money, not make enemies. Plus, this ad and commercial will be advertised locally at the new store on Avenue West. We want the right clientele coming in," Masterson said to them, and they agreed. Cader watched as Melise set the models up and fixed the clothing, positioned the woman coming in with her heels in her hand, ready to greet her boyfriend.

"Run this down again please," the producer asked, along with the assistant producer, and Cader watched her and listened, admiring her beauty and her vision.

"Okay, so the point is, he's standing there, all sexy, debonair in his amazing casual attire, barefoot, the shoes on the rim of the car where we can see them." She placed the model how she wanted him and the shoes so they could be seen, and then presented the scene. The ocean, the beach she would incorporate into the commercial. "And now comes his woman. One beautiful, classy, sexy woman. He looks at her, she smiles wide, heels in hand, and goes right to him. They embrace, she inhales against his neck, and bing, right-hand corner a bottle of your fragrance comes up, and where to purchase it, the website, and the name of the cologne," she said to them.

"So, one man, one woman?" the producer said.

"Yes. This line is about class and sophistication, not a Saturday night free for all, let's jump the hot guy with the great smelling cologne and cool clothes, then have sex in his back seat of the convertible before we get drunk and do it all over again. No," she rambled, and the producer laughed. So did Cader.

She exhaled. "Romantic, sexy, a capable man who can dress to perfection and smell incredible, too. That's what we women want," she said, and took hold of the model. "I want that kind of man. I want that focus on me," she pressed his cheek so the model looked down into her eyes, "and me only." She released him. "I'm not going to buy him something that makes him a sexual object to other women, no, he's mine, I'm his, and we are where it's all at because we wear this clothing and he wears that sexy cologne I love. That's why I choose this brand before any other."

Some of the extras began to clap, and the assistant produced whistled. "Love it!"

She looked at Cader, Sal, and Masterson, who smiled wide. "You got me sold, sweetheart."

"Me too," the male model told her. He pulled her into his arms and began to press his mouth to her neck, and everyone started laughing. She pushed away and gave his arm a light slap, and they all laughed.

"Let's do this," the producer said, and Cader was not only impressed, but interested, too.

* * * *

"So, what are the next steps?" Masterson asked her as they entered the restaurant, Carmichael's. She was feeling pretty good about things and about how the day had gone. She was way past Camille's attempts to sabotage the commercial. It looked great, and by the time she was done editing and adding little things to it through the software program, it would be awesome.

She felt his large hand at her lower back as he guided her to their table with the hostess, Cader and Sal in tow.

"Well, I'll get the final tapes from the producer, then upload everything into the program I use," she said as he pulled out her seat for her to take. She did, and they joined her. "Then I'll add additional touches, like putting the bottle of cologne at the bottom of the screen just so, and the website, as well. By the time it's released in just a few days, you should start seeing the results from the campaign. Of course, there are the print ads we'll run. You saw the copies I sent, right?" she asked, so excited, and by the way the three men stared at her, looking amused, she realized she was rambling.

She lowered her eyes and took a breath. "Sorry, I'm just so excited about the campaign and getting your products out there. I've been telling my friends about them, and they can't wait to go to the store to check out the cologne for their boyfriends."

"How about your boyfriend?" Cader asked her. Her cheeks went flush, her eyes widened, and she reached for the glass of water the busboy just poured for each of them.

"No boyfriend. Too busy," she said.

"Now that is a shame, but good news for me," Masterson said, and she looked at him and he licked his lower lip.

She felt a little uncomfortable, and it was obvious by her response. "I'm not Camille, Mr. Reynolds," she said very firmly.

He gazed over her body. "No, you sure the hell aren't," he replied.

The waitress came over to ask them what they wanted to drink, and he seemed annoyed. Simultaneously, Sal got a call on his cell phone and stood up to leave the room to take it. She took the time to pull herself together. These men were a lot older than her and definitely were the kind of men that didn't do commitments but one night stands. They were attractive, though, but it was the oddest thing when they asked about her having a boyfriend, that guy Jordan popped into her head. She knew nothing about Jordan, and only what her gut and her mind created. He may have been a soldier, since he had the Marine tattoo on his arm, but that wasn't enough to prove it. The reaction to the abrupt sound, indicated he might have PTSD, since he panicked and reacted like Elliott would. And the things he said about a bad side worried her, yet he was calm with her, and he loved her painting.

She gave him her painting. Jesus, what had she been thinking? It was his green eyes, that sexy grin, and all those muscles. He looked capable yet needy, and, of course, the long hair he had and his untamed look pulled at her feminine strings. She couldn't tame a man like Jordan. Or could she? She felt her cheeks warm, and then felt the hand on her arm, stroking her skin. She glanced to the left and locked gazes with Masterson. "I hope it was okay to order a bottle or two of wine for us. You like cabernet? It's a very good one."

"Oh, yes, definitely. Thank you," she said, refocusing. She needed to keep her mind on work and this business dinner, but then Sal returned, and he looked pissed.

"Sal?"

"We're going to have some company shortly. Merser and Dolinth are coming, along with some of their associates," he said to Masterson.

"Hmm, well, we are conducting business with Melise right now. Maybe we'll join them for a drink," Masterson said, and then looked back at Melise and gave her a wink.

"Other unexpected guests could be coming along, as well," Sal said, and Masterson looked concerned. "Check your cell," Sal continued, and at the same time, Cader looked at his cell phone.

"Will this be a problem?" Masterson asked.

"The jig is up," Sal said.

Masterson nodded. "Merser and Dolinth will take care of it," Masterson replied before he looked at Melise.

"Problem?" she asked.

"Not at all, beautiful. So, tell us more about yourself. What do you like to do when you aren't working?" he asked.

She didn't want to lead them on or make them believe she would be interested in them. "I think we should stick to talking business. That is what all this is about? Promoting your products. Why don't you tell me about this new location for the grand opening? I thought my boss, Mr. LaGrange, mentioned that it's in Trenton," she said, and then took a sip from her wine glass.

"Hmmm, playing hard to get, I see. We'll work on that."

"Mr. Reynolds—"

"Masterson, unless you prefer sir, but if you dare call me that, be prepared for my reaction." She felt his palm glide along her knee and slightly under the hem of her dress. She covered his hand.

"Masterson, I thought I mentioned that I wasn't Camille," she said, voice nearly cracking. She was shaking and felt Cader's arm go around the back of her chair as his fingers slid along her neck under her hair.

"Oh baby, we know you aren't her. Camille would have done us in the back of the SUV on the way over here. Hell, she would have offered her body at the shoot," Cader said, and she gulped.

She pushed Masterson's hand off her knee and shrugged her shoulders, pulling from Cader's touch. "Then realize I'm not part of the package or contract with Wayworth Industries. In fact, I don't really need to be here right now," she stated.

"You've offended her, and that wasn't our intention," Sal said from across the table. She stared at him as Masterson and Cader gave her space.

"Let's enjoy a nice dinner together, a celebration of the job well done. I'll also notify the department to send some samples of things to your home, so your friends can sample the products for their boyfriends," Masterson told her.

"That isn't necessary."

"No, it is. A gesture of apology for insulting you," Masterson told her.

"We moved too quickly. You aren't what we're used to, and that interests us more," Cader said.

The waitress returned with their food orders, and then the men ran the conversation and she was grateful. As the evening went on and they finished their meals, they asked her to join them at the bar. It was only her second glass of wine, and she knew she would need a ride back to the studio for her car, but she was thinking she might call a car service instead.

"There they are," Cader spoke while they were at a table by the bar now. She saw five men approach in dark suits with intense expressions, and her heart began to race. As their jackets parted, she spotted the guns in holsters and knew they were made men, but who?

"Have you been to the storefront?" one man asked Masterson as they shook hands hello.

"Not this week, but definitely tomorrow. I hear the construction is coming along perfectly with the surrounding structures, though."

"Yes, indeed." The man looked at Melise. He gazed over her body and reached for her hand. "And who is this gorgeous young woman?" he asked, and she took in the sight of the man. Late forties, black and grey hair, stocky, yet wealthy. The other man next to him eating her up with his eyes had a thinner built but was close to his same age, the other three were security. Definitely security, as they took position with their backs toward them and their eyes on the exits and the people in the bar area.

"Merser Volcheck, and Dolinth Ferchosky, meet Melise Minter, from Wayworth Industries."

"Ahh, the woman with all the creative ideas, and creative positions?" he inquired and slid his hand to her waist.

She stepped back, and Masterson pulled her closer to him as he chuckled. "No, you're thinking of Camille."

"Ah, my mistake. So sorry, Melise. It's hard to keep up with the many women who throw themselves at my business associates. After all, Masterson, Cader, and Sal are quite the catch, don't you think?" he asked.

"I'm only doing business with them, Mr. Volcheck, so I wouldn't know. I like to keep things professional," she replied, and he squinted at her, but then Dolinth reached his hand out.

"Well, maybe we can change your mind and you'll enjoy our company instead," he said to her, completely flirting and acting like she would throw herself at these men because of their power, and their money.

She chuckled. "I'm going to call it a night. I have a big commercial to work on in the morning, and I want to be clear headed." She went to place her wine glass down, but Cader stopped her.

"Finish the drink with us. No need to run off," Cader told her. She held it there as the men began to discuss some kind of warehouse and distribution center she assumed had something to do with the products they were storing and then shipping out to customers. Both Cader and Masterson remained close to her, a hand each at her lower back as they spoke about the company and about other items being stored in a warehouse or something on site. They weren't being specific about the other items.

She felt out of place, and then saw two of the guards block some people from coming toward them. She couldn't see past the tall men, but then felt Masterson's breath against her ear and neck. "Just stay close and I'll keep you safe. These men coming in are nothing but trouble. Merser and Dolinth deal with them."

She was instantly worried. "Listen, I'm going to get going. I don't need to be in the middle of some business transaction I'm not even a part of. I appreciate dinner and—"

He pulled her closer just as she recognized the voice. Her heart felt like it stopped beating as she turned and saw Pelham Marquis, along with Carson and Warren. They didn't look happy, and the guards that were with Merser and his buddy looked on edge.

"Stay next to me. These men are animals. They kill people," Masterson whispered to her and she was definitely scared. She knew them, knew that the Marquis brothers were made men, were dangerous and capable, but killers? Oh God, she really needed to get the hell out of here.

She started to push down on Masterson's grip, and he released her. "I'm going to get out of here," she said, but then turned and locked gazes with Pelham, and holy shit, he was furious.

"Melise?"

"What the fuck are you doing here and with men like these?" Carson asked, stepping closer, but Masterson pulled her back, and Cader and Sal took position by her, too.

"You know these men?" Merser asked her, his expression unreadable.

"Yes, I do, but I don't know what's going on exactly here, and I think I should get going."

Masterson grabbed her hand. "We drove you here, we'll bring you back to the studio for your car," he said to her, and then reached up to stroke her jaw. Why did she feel like he did that to piss of Pelham?

"Not necessary. Obviously, you have other business to discuss and our business ended hours ago. Have a good night," she said and began walking away.

"She doesn't have a car, and you men have interrupted our celebration," Masterson said to Pelham.

"She's a big girl, I'm sure she can handle getting a ride. Now, let's discuss a few things, shall we?" she heard Pelham say before she hurried out of there. She didn't know what to do or who to call, and then decided that an Uber would be her best bet. She logged into the app and put in the information, but no one was around for fifteen minutes. When a large hand grabbed her upper arm and started bringing her toward the side of the building, she protested until she realized who it was.

"Jordan?" she asked, sounding breathless to her own ears. "What are you doing here? Why did you grab me?" she asked, but he didn't respond.

He hit unlock on some dark SUV and then opened the back door. "Get inside and don't say a word."

She pulled her arm free. "Wait, why? What is this all about?" she asked him. He was breathing through his nostrils, and he looked ready to fight.

"Volcheck and Ferchosky. How do you fucking know them? And don't lie to me. I don't know where you came from, how you're involved with this, or if it's some kind of set up against my brothers and me and Costanza."

"Wait, your brothers? Who?"

"Get her in the car." Warren appeared, and Carson was getting in on the other side while Pelham got in on the passenger side.

"Get in the car, Melise," Jordan commanded.

"Jordan."

"Now," He lifted her up and deposited her into the backseat like she weighed nothing at all. He slammed the door closed and then got into the driver's side and started to drive. She didn't know what was going on and felt more confused as they argued about how Jordan knew her, about meeting her by the pier, and it being a setup.

"Oh my God, what are you even talking about?" she asked as tears filled her eyes. When Warren reached out his hand to grab her arm, she gasped. Tears fell. "Please don't kill me."

"What?" Pelham yelled from the front seat, and she jumped.

"Calm down. We aren't going to kill you, Melise. Just relax. Calm your breathing. We have questions," Jordan said, and she could tell that he was annoyed still. She swallowed hard and took a deep breath, but as she looked at Warren and Carson, saw the guns on their waists and their angry expressions, it was too difficult not to shake. When the SUV stopped somewhere and both Pelham and Jordan got out, Warren and Carson remained with her and the doors closed, she really started to shake. Then she heard the yelling.

"You fucking met her and you didn't say a word to us? They could be using her to get to us, do you realize that, Jordan?" Pelham yelled.

"Ask her the fucking questions, Pelham. You want me to hold the fucking gun to her head and do it, I will."

"No. What the fuck?"

"I'm just as pissed off and shocked as you are, Pelham."

"Not as shocked as I am. As Carson and Warren are to learn that you met Melise, spent time with her, and she's friends with these assholes. You know what Merser and Dolinth are into, and you saw the way they kept her close. What the fuck?" Pelham yelled.

"Get her out of there and ask her," Jordan said. She heard the whole conversation, and Carson and Warren watched her like they didn't trust her. The door opened and she tightened up, expecting to be pulled out and roughed up, or whatever gangsters did to people they didn't trust or who they thought were double-crossing them. She didn't do anything.

She looked around them and had no idea where they were. Somewhere that was dark, but she thought she could smell water. Maybe the bay.

Pelham's nostrils flared. His hands were on his hips, his green eyes looked evil, and the gun on his hip warned her to obey him. "How do you know those men?"

"Which ones?"

"All of them," Carson snapped at her from right behind her. He and Warren were close to her, she felt the heat of their bodies. She never felt such intimidation in her life.

"I work for Wayworth Industries, and we have a contract with Masterson, Cader, and Sal and their line of products for men. I was with them all day at a photo shoot, and I'll be creating their ads and commercials for their products. I was asked to go to dinner with them tonight and discuss further ideas.

"I never met Merser and Dolinth until this evening. I didn't even want to go because my boss, Mr. Wayworth, hinted about keeping Mr. Reynolds and his associates happy and I wasn't sure what he meant. Suddenly, they were hitting on me, and I was declining their offers so they would know I wasn't like Camille, and then the next thing I know those other men show up, and they start flirting. I tried to leave, and they wouldn't let me yet, and then you came. I know nothing else, just heard them talking about a warehouse or something and other products, and it sounded like not the products for men but something else. I was going to leave and—"

She squeaked as Carson slid his arm around her waist and pressed up against her back. "Masterson had his arm around your waist. The three of them were keeping you close and acting possessive like you belong to them," Carson whispered into her ear.

She shook her head as more tears fell. "No, Carson, I don't belong to anyone. I told them I didn't have a boyfriend, and I work a lot, and oh God, please, don't hurt me."

Pelham cursed, closed the space between them, wrapped his arm around her waist, and hugged her to him.

* * * *

Pelham was more scared for Melise than angry at her. She hadn't a clue what she was in the middle of, or what her profession caused her to get involved in. That storefront was a front for other things—drugs, stolen merchandise, and a pick-up and drop off location for deals. The thing that concerned him the most and really made him pissed off, as well as jealous, was how those men all looked at Melise, wanting her. She was too damn sweet and naive to even know it.

He glanced at Jordan, who was clenching his teeth and ready to kick ass. Pelham inhaled Melise's perfume, the scent of her hair, and caressed her back, and then her ass as she shook. She had a great ass, and while he gave it a squeeze and she slowly pulled away, he lost the ability to keep his distance. Those gorgeous green eyes, the tears on her thick lashes, and her full, quivering lips were too much to ignore. He pressed his mouth to hers and kissed her. When she tightened up and he heard Warren's voice, he knew his brother joined in.

"You're so damn sweet, you hadn't a fucking clue, and that pisses me off, Melise. They could have hurt you, seduced you, and fucking forced you to..." Warren didn't complete his sentence as Pelham released her lips and Warren turned her to face him, kissing her next. Gripping her hair, Warren explored her body with his hands. He cupped her ass and lifted her snugger against his body, when he finally released her lips, she was holding onto his arms and trying to catch her breath.

She looked fuckable, with those full lips, that shocked expression, but then Carson slid in behind her, wrapped his arm around her waist and suckled against her neck. "You need protection. How could you not know they were dangerous?" he asked.

"Dangerous?" she asked, her eyes locked with Jordan's. "Like a dark side?" she said, and Pelham didn't know what she was talking about, but obviously Jordan did. His chest tightened, his heart raced as Jordan stepped closer. The idea that his brother, so distant, so troubled, could share an attraction to Melise like they had for her was a miracle. He felt like he was holding his breath as Jordan reached out and cupped her cheek and jaw, then closed the space between them.

"Didn't I warn you about the dangers out there at night?" he asked.

"On the beach. You said the beach." Her voice cracked. She was definitely scared.

"Everywhere. Evil lurks in the darkness just waiting for innocent, sweet, prey like you. I'm so angry with you, Melise," he told her and traced her jaw with his index finger.

"I didn't know. I swear, it was a business dinner, and then it just happened."

"They could have hurt you."

"They didn't though. You guys got there. You made sure to get me to safety."

"You think you're safe with us? With me?" he asked, once again teeth clenched, and Pelham was worried that his brother could lose his cool. Could have an episode and scare the crap out of Melise.

"Should I not feel safe?" she asked.

"You shouldn't be here, be involved in any of this. If we didn't know you, I would have put a gun to your head and forced information from you. Do you get that?" He raised his voice, and she trembled. Pelham could tell.

"But you do know me, Jordan."

He released her jaw. He didn't kiss her, and Pelham was disappointed. He hoped Melise could be something deeper to connect them all. Something special.

"How do we get her uninvolved with this?" Jordan asked Pelham, putting distance between him and Melise.

"We don't. They now know we know her and are protective of her. They're interested in her, and she needs to do her job," Pelham said, though he couldn't help but be upset and concerned.

"Those men screw women left and right. They'll get to her," Warren added.

"Not if we protect her and set some rules," Pelham added, gazing over her body.

"What do you mean, rules?" she asked them.

They were silent, and Pelham was trying to read his brothers. He knew Carson and Warren were on board here to protect Melise, but anything more would be an unwise assumption. Then there was Jordan, currently in a dead stare at Melise, looking suspicious and on edge.

Pelham was right in front of her. "You know who we are? What we do for a living, or at minimum, who we do business with, don't you?" She shook her head. "Words," he commanded.

"Not really, Pelham, and I don't need to know. I mean, I understand from being friends with Sue, Nina, London, and Francesca that they don't ask questions when it comes to business. I know it seemed like I could have been part of something, but I wasn't," she replied.

"You shouldn't be around men like that," Jordan stated firmly.

"Yeah, well, it wasn't like I planned it, Jordan, okay?"

"Not okay. We don't know what the reaction or the consequences of tonight might bring your way and ours," Pelham said.

"Consequences? Like what?"

"Merser and Dolinth are criminals and businessmen who would sell their own sister to make a profit. Both of them also love to get things, things that they're told they can't have." He looked her body over.

She placed her hand against her neck. "You mean like sell me off as some sex slave, or take me away and send me to places like they did to my friends? Oh God, they're into that? Oh God." She was totally panicking.

Carson gripped her shoulders from behind her. "Calm down. They aren't into human trafficking, but they are known to force their way into women's lives and their beds. They're drug dealers, thieves that resell stolen merchandise on the black market or to specific buyers. Bad stuff but profitable," Carson explained to her.

"Profitable? So, you're involved with those things, too?" she asked.

"Heed your friends' warnings about not asking questions," Pelham reminded her.

"I want to go home. I won't tell anyone about tonight. I'll deal with those men best I can without losing my job," she said with pleading eyes, glossy and emotional.

"That may not be so easy, but let's not assume and see what happens. What you'll need to do is keep in contact with us. You notice anything strange, anyone following you, or anyone pushing for information on us, anything, you get in touch with us," Pelham told her.

Carson slid his hands down her arms and then around her waist, hugging her from behind. He kissed her neck. "You should plan on seeing us again, on a less dangerous level," he whispered.

She tilted her head to the side, her eyes closed. "Do you think that's a good idea? Perhaps we should stay away from one another."

"Not happening," Warren stated before Carson could.

"Carson," she whispered, but then Warren stepped closer, cupped her cheeks, and began to kiss her. Carson slid her hands behind her back, and she moaned into Warren's mouth. Pelham looked at Jordan, who remained watching them, then glanced at Pelham.

"We'll handle it," Pelham said to him.

"We'd better."

Chapter 4

"What do you mean, Melise was there when you confronted them?" Costanza asked.

"Apparently, the company Melise works for represents Masterson, Cader, and Sal's company and their products. She was working with them on a commercial earlier in the day. I don't really know, but what I do know is that all of those men wanted her. Seeing us arrive, showing that we know Melise may have just put her further on their radar."

"Son of a bitch. She's lucky you guys were there tonight. We know how these men operate and the kind of shit they would pull on a woman, never mind one like Melise. She's sweet, maybe a bit naive."

"Oh, believe me, we were pissed. All of us."

"All of you?" Costanza asked, leaning back in his chair as Pelham held his gaze. He didn't say anything a moment. "What?"

"Jordan met Melise before."

Costanza's eyes widened. "How? Where?"

"The pier a few nights ago. I didn't get the details, but the gist of it I gathered from their response to one another, and clearly they hit it off. Jordan's upset. Neither knew who the other was."

"That's awesome. You don't need to hold back pursuing Melise now. That was your worry when we discussed things at the party."

"We made moves. He didn't, but I could tell he was pissed, that he wanted to hold her, to kiss her, but he was holding back. You know he still has those episodes every so often, and last night I feared he could lose it over his concern for Melise. He's holding back."

"You know why. He still thinks he isn't good enough or right enough because of the weakness those episodes bring on. He'll pull through. Look how far he's come in the last year," Costanza said.

"I know, believe me, Costanza, I know. We made a lot of changes. We don't do so much of this muscling around shit like we used to. That's always helped him deal with his need to get out any feelings of anxiousness and anger. But last night, he didn't sleep well at all. Was up, in the gym, then went for a run, then back into the gym until he exhausted himself."

"Sounds like he really cares about Melise, is attracted to her. Where did you leave things off?"

"For her to call us if anything happened, like she felt she was being watched, or any of those men approached her, asked questions. We talked to her about getting together, about being aware of her surroundings, everything."

"Good. So, how much longer does she need to work with these men?"

"I don't know. We didn't discuss it. She was pretty shaken up, but she pulled it together. There's a toughness to her, you know. I'm sure having her friends, like Nina, involved with you guys, with men like us, helps her to have a bit of an understanding."

"I'm sure. I can have Nina talk to her, as well, although they are probably already talking about things."

Pelham held his gaze and didn't smile. He exhaled, his heart heavy. His concern and protective feelings over Melise were making him think about her right now.

"Hey, it will work out."

"Costanza, we know these men. We showed concern of Melise last night, and it was pretty fucking clear that we were jealous. These fucks will use that. You know they will."

"It doesn't matter. They need to pay up. They should be kissing our asses for not losing our shit on them for keeping their business under wraps and not paying for use of the territory. They want to push, they'll suffer."

"You should have seen the way they looked at Melise, and how Masterson pulled her close, a protective stance, and the others blocked us from her."

"They would be foolish to do anything stupid. However, Merser and Dolinth are the ones bringing in the stolen merchandise and drugs. Masterson and his buddies are providing the cover storefronts. Their product line is established elsewhere, and that's their money pit. They bought out the shopping center and warehouse as a location to launder their money and to distribute and store."

"What are you saying? They could seduce her and pretend to be all legit business-men?" Pelham asked, on the defensive. Costanza raised one of his eyebrows at Pelham as if saying, "Yeah, pretty much."

"Fuck," Pelham said on an exhale.

"Make your move."

"Like we're any better with what we're involved in? What do we have to offer her when we don't do commitments? When Jordan backed away and has his issues he's trying to deal with?"

"So, you're going to just sit back and watch those dicks or fucking men like Merser and Dolinth make moves on your woman? You're okay with them kissing her, touching her, hell, fucking her?"

"No."

"Then what's the fucking problem, man?" Costanza asked him.

Pelham was breathing through his nostrils. The thought of any other men, especially those five, touching Melise or getting her in their beds made his see red. "Jordan."

"You said he met her and showed interest. He'll come around."

"If he doesn't, we won't commit to her."

"You'll send her to the fucking wolves, and you're okay with that? I don't fucking think so. You're like me, like my brothers were before Nina. No commitments, no vulnerability or fucking bullshit. Then, we see the danger she's in, the pain she's in, and learn about that dick who raped her, abused her, and it sent us over the edge, and we couldn't fight the attraction or the need to protect her."

"I didn't say I wouldn't protect her. Even Jordan wants that."

"If you're not ready, not willing to change things and commit to her, then at least make sure she's safe. But if you push her away, show no interest in taking it to that intimate level, she's single and fair game. To any men. How does that make you guys and Jordan feel?"

* * * *

Melise was sitting at her computer station working hard on trying to complete the commercial for Masterson, Cader, and Sal. It was almost complete, and then she would present it to her bosses and the men at a meeting in a couple of hours. She was nervous about seeing them again after last night. She hadn't heard from Pelham, Carson, Warren, or Jordan even, despite exchanging cell phone numbers. She thought about what she knew or heard about the men. Heavies, men who beat people up to get what they wanted, or even killed. Businessmen in both criminal and legit activities. They owned various real estate properties, buildings, a marina, and storefronts with Costanza and his brothers. They were wealthy and powerful, and they seemed fast, like commitments to a woman wouldn't be something they'd want.

But when she thought about how protective they acted, how concerned for her, and how deeply they kissed her, none of that mattered or seemed right. That was in the midst of being scared, the adrenaline pumping and the sexual attraction high. Now, calmer, rational, she realized that they weren't the right men for her.

She was normal, boring, typical, and longed for love, passion, a connection so deep nothing else mattered but being with that person and living life together. Jordan couldn't even kiss her. It was like he knew his brothers were just taking what they wanted and there wouldn't be that commitment. She allowed it. Their powerful, dominant attitudes drew her in and grabbed a hold of her libido and took off. She was stupid and easy last night, and she couldn't let that happen again.

She hit play on the keyboard, her headset on, and she watched the finalized commercial. Naturally, her gaze went to the model, the focal point of the commercial. He was handsome, funny, and he even asked her out. She chuckled. A model might be safer than a gangster or four, but maybe not. The blonde had given her looks, but a guy as sexy and good-looking, who modeled, would definitely not wind up with a regular woman like her.

When the cologne bottle appeared, and she took in the sight of the designer clothing, the sexy, debonair look, and the feel of the model portraying such a character, she wondered if someone like that would be the better choice? Someone professional, trying to make a name for himself. But Masterson, Cader, and Sal had at least fifteen years on her, and they did know Merser and Dolinth, who were criminals. She just didn't seem to be able to attract the right man, or men. She should focus back on work and pray that Masterson wouldn't be angry she declined lunch today to discuss so-called business.

She jumped when the hand landed on her shoulder. Eleanor laughed and so did Melise.

"That good, huh?" Eleanor asked and looked at the model on the screen.

"Makes me want to buy the cologne," Melise said and smiled.

"If it comes with that model or even the sports car, I'm in," Eleanor said to her and raised her eyebrows up and down, making Melise chuckle. "Well, once you meet with Mr. Reynolds and crew presenting the finalized commercial, you won't have to meet them again."

"I don't know about that. Seems they are quite impressed with her," Camille interrupted, walking into the room. Melise removed the headset from around her neck.

"I understand you made some changes. Big ones to the commercial. Why wasn't I informed or asked for an approval?" Camille asked.

"Mr. Masterson and his associates were there and they approved and loved the ideas. The commercial came out fantastic, Camille. The clients will be more than satisfied."

"Oh, I know they will be when I present the commercial to them. So send me the finalized copy."

Melise knew what Camille was doing. She was going to take all the credit for the commercial and its creation despite knowing that the clients were aware that Melise did it herself. Before Melise could say anything, Eleanor chimed in.

"Too late, Camille. The final copy has gone out, credits to producers, actors, and creative designer and director were labeled, giving credit to those who actually did their job. Melise will be gaining quite the following for the company."

"You can't do that without my approval. I'm supposed to look at everything before it goes to the clients and Mr. Wayworth." Camille raised her voice.

"Hmmm, maybe in the past, but not since a conversation between all three bosses and Mr. Masterson last night."

"Last night?" Camille asked, and smoothed her hands along her hips.

"Yes, I don't know what was exchanged between them, but Mr. Wayworth was furious. He should be in shortly, but the meeting with the clients is going to occur."

"Well, I should get things ready, then. I know what Mr. Reynolds expects," she said and walked out of the room.

"What in the world was that all about?" Melise asked Eleanor.

Eleanor looked over her shoulder and then whispered to Melise, "I got a call from Beth, Wayworth's secretary, and she said she overheard a conversation between Mr. Wayworth and Mr. Reynolds. Camille showed up at their penthouse to have sex with them, and she bad-mouthed you. Said you destroyed the commercial."

"What?" Melise felt her cheeks go red and her heart race.

"I know, crazy bitch thinks she can spread her legs and get whatever she wants. I think it backfired on her, because she's sleeping with all three bosses here."

"Did she sleep with Masterson and them?"

"Why, interested?" Eleanor asked, and Melise gave her a sideways expression. Eleanor snickered. "They are super-hot men and loaded. Oh, they wanted your address to drop off boxes of samples or something."

Melise's gut clenched. "What?"

"I hope it was okay that we gave them your address. Mr. Masterson's secretary said that you all discussed it at dinner. Your friends were interested in the cologne for their men?" she asked. Melise released a sigh remembering that she did say that.

"Oh God, I did mention that. When are they delivering it?"

"I think today."

"Okay."

"Why do you look so worried, Melise?"

"Camille is going to be pissed, and she'll blame me for all of this."

"No way she can do anything, the bosses are more pissed probably because she cheated on them, or attempted to. The woman is greedy, and she's caused a lot of problems here. You've been here for two years and have seen some things, but I've been here ten and the number of women she's chased out of here or destroyed their careers is sickening. It only got worse when she finally got into bed with the bosses. I hope they fire her ass. She doesn't do anything anyway," Eleanor said, then glanced at her watch. "You'd better get ready."

Melise nodded and then checked the thumb drive to make sure the commercial was saved, and nothing could be done to destroy it, then logged off the program. She was going to head to the meeting room a little early to set the computers up, and she was definitely nervous. She didn't trust Camille one bit, and all she wanted to do was put last night behind her and just work on another account and get lost in painting over the weekend.

* * * *

"Again Masterson, I'm so sorry about the situation last night. Camille will be dealt with accordingly," Mr. Wayworth said to him.

Masterson nodded his head. "If it weren't for Melise, I would have considered pulling the contract. She's professional, and she came in there yesterday and redid the entire commercial. I can't wait to see the final result of that hard work."

"Yes, I've heard it's outstanding, and she's always so professional, so I wouldn't expect anything less."

"The woman deserves a bonus and then some," Cader added, and Mr. Wayworth nodded.

"Shall we head into the meeting room? I believe that Camille has set everything up with Melise."

"Camille is in there with Melise?" Sal asked, and Masterson was concerned. That Camille was a piece of work and very jealous of Melise.

As they got to the door, she could hear Camille reprimanding Melise. Melise's eyes went immediately to them and to her bosses as they joined them.

"This is why I'm in charge. You lost the commercial, accidentally deleted the final copy. It will take days to pull all the pieces together and start over. Wait until they hear about this. Then you won't look so perfect to them," Camille said, her voice raised. "I bet you had something to do with this. Just like how you've sabotaged other women who you felt threatened by," Melise told her.

"How dare you? I can destroy you, Melise. You think I can't? You think I haven't begun to change things in the computer system or haven't messed with your projects, hell, your money?"

"That's enough!" Mr. Wayworth barked.

"I'll call security," Mr. LaGrange stated.

"Camille, remove yourself from this meeting. You're done here."

"Done? I'm not done. She's done." Camille stepped toward Melise, but Cader and Sal were already next to her, pulling her behind them.

"You have problems, and you need to leave. Do yourself a favor and stay clear of Melise, or you'll be dealing with us. You don't know who we know," Sal said to her. Camille growled and stomped her foot as security escorted her from the room.

"Are you okay?" Cader asked Melise, caressing her arms.

She exhaled. "She's lost her mind," she whispered, and Cader pulled her into his arms and hugged her.

Masterson hid his grin and looked at Mr. Wayworth. "I hope you will do as you said and handle this. That woman shouldn't have even been here. Melise deserves better treatment than this."

"Of course she does, and we know that if anything pops up, problems or accusations, they are false and are not initiated by Melise. Camille will be dealt with."

Melise stepped from Cader's embrace as Sal caressed her cheek with his knuckles. "Okay?" he asked, and she nodded.

"I'm fine. I'm sorry about this situation, Mr. Reynolds."

"Masterson. Come on, Melise," he reprimanded.

She nibbled her bottom lip.

"Is it true? Did she delete the final copy of the commercial?" Gary Fort, her other boss, asked.

"Seriously?" Sal asked, looking annoyed.

"No need to worry. I try to plan ahead and not take any chances, especially for clients as import as Masterson, Sal, and Cader." She held up the thumb drive.

"Thank God," Louis LaGrange said, and they started to take their seats around the table.

* * * *

Melise couldn't help but to smile when everyone clapped at the end of the commercial. Despite the crazy confrontation with Camille, it all went well. They shook hands good-bye, her bosses and the others leaving the room, leaving her with Masterson, Cader, and Sal.

"I loved it, Melise. We're so impressed. You know the storefront the new store will be opening in?" he asked.

"Yes."

"I take it you know how those friends of yours operate, then?" he asked.

She was immediately uncomfortable. "I don't know what you mean."

"Sure you do, and to be honest, we were a bit upset finding out that you were friends with such men," Sal added.

"I really don't know what you mean. I've only known the Marquis brothers for a short period of time."

"They're bullies, made men forcing their way into our pockets," Cader said with attitude. She scrunched her eyes.

"You don't know what they do, do you?" Masterson asked, in a reprimanding tone.

"It isn't any of my business. I left last night because I didn't belong there. There's no need to tell me any of this." She went to turn, but Masterson grabbed her arm and pulled her close. She gasped and stared up into his eyes.

"You should know that they force people to pay them money and call it protection. The more the store brings in, the more 'protection' the store gets."

She didn't know why he was telling her this. She remembered what Pelham and his brothers told her about Masterson and the others being dangerous. "I don't want any trouble, Masterson. It isn't any of my business."

His hold tightened. She could feel his palm over her lower back practically to her ass. "Don't be naive. You're sweet, young, and unknowing to such violent criminal minds like those men. We were worried about you last night. How you disappeared. If we had known where you lived, we would have come by to ensure that you were okay." He reached up and caressed her hair from her cheek.

She pushed down on his arms. "Please Masterson, release me. It's not appropriate."

"Because you're working for us, you mean?" Cader asked. He and Sal were right there, too, and she was a bit scared, yet she knew she hadn't done anything to make them angry or to hurt them so that they would want to hurt her.

"Yes." She looked past him and toward the door. It was closed, though.

"We're almost done here. No need for any other meetings or anything for a bit. Come out with us. Get to know who we really are," Masterson said to her. She pushed a little more and he released her. She stepped back.

"I can't. I don't get involved with clients, and I actually don't date. I have a lot on my plate."

"We'll give you a little time, but we want to take you to dinner without interruptions from gangsters and their threats."

She wondered if he was telling the truth and maybe Pelham and his brothers were fudging the truth in a way. After all, what did she really know about them but hearsay? And Jordan? Well, he just closed up on her and didn't even make a move to kiss her or show affection. They might have been pissed off that she was a witness to what they really do. Force money from business owners. It made sense.

"You're smart, Melise, I'm sure you can see what's really happening. If you see those men again, be careful, a sweet woman like you would get eaten alive. They don't respect women, they use them." He stepped away from her. "Let's go," he said to Sal and Cader. She watched them exit the room. Her head beginning to throb, and her heart ached a little with confusion. She would be smarter to stay away from all of them.

* * * *

"What do you think?" Sal asked Masterson.

"I think she'll keep her distance from them, but also from us. That's something we'll need to work on. It would be smarter to have her willingly choose us and not force it, but I know Merser and Dolinth will want to use her to get the Marquis men and Lopez men off our asses. No need to give them so much money just because we're doing business in the area. Our other plan will work."

"Camille is a crazy bitch. I think if we weren't there with Wayworth, she would have struck Melise," Cader said to them.

"I don't doubt that, but we do know that Melise goes to the martial arts and kickboxing gym. Keep that car on her, too. Merser wants to know who she meets, where she goes, how accessible she is, so you know how that works."

"Merser and Dolinth are only interested in Melise to use her to keep the Marquis brothers at bay. Those guys are pretty fucking ruthless, though, and some fine piece of ass is not going to stop them from doing what they want," Cader said as they exited the building.

* * * *

Melise had gotten the text messages from her brother Ben saying that he, Phoenix, and Elliott were heading to Corporals for drinks. She was glad that Elliott was feeling better. His episodes came in stages, but this last one concerned her. She had put a call in to Kiana, who was willing to meet Elliott and talk to him, but Elliott was not even willing to meet and talk to her.

She had texted back that she would be there in about twenty minutes. She was dressed nicely, a bit overly dressed for the bar, but after the emotional day at work, she knew if she headed home she would probably shower and put on a t-shirt and sweats and watch TV in the bedroom. She pulled into the parking lot a short time later, reapplied her lip gloss, and then got out of her car. She spotted her three big brothers immediately and smiled wide as they each embraced her. They headed inside and she saw a bunch of people she knew. They said their hellos and then caught seats at the bar.

"How was your work week?" Ben asked her, then took a sip from his mug of beer as he watched a few blondes walk by. He was leaning back against the bar, and Elliott and Phoenix were right next to her as she sat on the stool.

"Tiresome. I am so looking forward to the weekend."

"You working on something big?" Phoenix asked her.

"Finishing up a new account and a commercial for it. Products for men. Clothing, cologne."

"Stupid shit?" Ben asked.

"No, actually, the owners will be opening up a storefront in Trenton," she explained.

"Sounds cool, I guess, but not really my thing. Maybe Ben's. He's into fashion now," Elliott teased, and they chuckled. She loved seeing them like this and seeing Elliott a lot calmer.

As they talked about work and she told them about the shoot and Camille, they grew more annoyed. "She could make you lose your job? Seriously?" Elliott asked.

"Not anymore. She got fired today, security escorted her out." As she explained, she noticed Phoenix staring at someone or something behind her.

She reached out and touched his arm. "What's wrong?"

He stood straighter. "Some fucking guy is staring at you and us, and he looks psycho."

"What?" she asked and turned to look as Elliott and Ben did, too. She was shocked to see Jordan standing there, and even more shocked when his eyes widened and Elliott turned toward him.

"Jordan?" Elliott said, and Jordan came closer.

"Elliott? Holy fuck." The two men embraced, and Melise looked at Ben and Phoenix as Jordan and Elliott pulled back and were talking to one another.

"I can't believe you're here. You live around here?" Elliott asked Jordan.

"Yeah, been here for over two years now. How about you?"

"Yeah, I live in town," he said. Elliott placed his arm over Melise's shoulder and pulled her next to him, and she saw Jordan's eyes darken. "This is my sister, Melise, my two brothers, Ben and Phoenix."

"Sister?" Jordan said, and Elliott looked at Melise.

"You know Jordan?" he asked her.

"We know one another. Have some friends in similar circles," she said. Jordan stepped closer to shake hands with Ben and Phoenix. She couldn't believe this. They knew one another, had served together in the Marine Corps.

"Are you still working with your brothers?" Jordan asked him.

She swallowed hard as the two men continued to speak. She caught Phoenix and Ben looking at her and knew they would question her later. Then as they talked, she realized that if Jordan did suffer from PTSD and was more like the type of guy to not socialize and definitely not hang out at bars, then why was he here? He was obviously shocked to see her brother, and he was angry seeing her with these three men, not knowing they were her brothers. As she processed her thoughts it hit her. *He followed me here? Oh God, he was going to follow me home if I went there. What if he is as dangerous as Masterson and them said? Oh God.*

When she felt a hand on her hip, she tightened up and looked right up at Jordan. He stared down into her eyes. Her brothers were right there watching.

"I can't believe you're Elliott's sister. He met Pelham, Carson, and Warren before, too," he told her, like that was supposed to ease her mind.

"Small world," she said, kind of snappy.

"How did you guys meet?" Ben asked Jordan as he looked at him and Melise.

"Just through friends. He and his brothers know Costanza and his brothers," Melise told them.

"That was crazy what happened to your friend Nina. Thank God those guys know so many people and they were able to find her," Ben said. Jordan remained close, and they all continued to talk. He was caressing her hips, and she was getting used to his size, to having him so close. Her brother Phoenix gave her a wink, and she knew she blushed. She couldn't help it. She wanted to be angry, annoyed, accusatory, but with each caress of his hand against her waist, those feelings minimized, and desire grew.

* * * *

"She's at a bar with three men and Jordan. What do you want to do?"

"Three men and Jordan? Do you mean Pelham, Carson, and Warren Marquis?" Masterson asked.

"No. Different guys. They greeted her with kisses to her cheek and were doing a lot of talking. When Jordan showed up, one of the guys knew him."

"Stick with her. Follow her home to see if she goes with all of them."

"Got it."

Masterson ended the call and rubbed his chin. Was she really falling for Jordan Marquis? He was the one Merser said was violent and thought nothing of killing. He also laid low and barely went out. This was good information for Merser and Dolinth that they could use as leverage to get payments down, but for Masterson, Cader, and Sal, it meant they might not have a chance with her. It annoyed him more than he thought that possibility would. But business was business, and he had to do what the bosses ordered.

* * * *

"It was nice talking to you and hanging out, man. We'll have to do it again," Phoenix said to Jordan as he shook his hand. Melise remained back next to Ben.

"Definitely a nice surprise. Melise, I'll see you around," Jordan said to her, and she thought he might kiss her cheek or something, but he didn't. He was doing that distance thing again. She exhaled and watched him leave.

"He's a good guy but into dangerous shit. You want to follow in your friends' footsteps?" Ben asked her.

"I don't know what you mean," she said, looking away, but Jordan already disappeared.

"You damn well know what I mean. He likes you, you like him. His brothers want you, too?" Ben asked.

"Ben." She lowered her eyes, and he placed his arm over her shoulder as they walked through the bar toward the door.

"You don't date, you're working all the time, taking care of us, of Mom and Dad, and helping Elliott. It's okay to want a personal life."

"I know that. It's just, well…complicated."

"Because he has PTSD like I do?" Elliott chimed in as they exited the building.

"Elliott."

"No. Is that why you're not reciprocating the attraction?" Elliott asked her.

"No, I don't even know if he has it or not."

"You know. You've been around me enough," Elliott replied.

"I just don't know if he's right for me, and work right now just got complicated with those clients and Camille."

"What are they, good-looking, wealthy clients who want you, too?" Phoenix asked and chuckled. When she remained straight-faced, he narrowed his eyes. "Seriously? Who are they? Have they tried something?"

She knew she couldn't tell them about the conversation she overheard at the restaurant and the business between Merser and the Marquis brothers.

"It doesn't matter, I'm not willing to take a chance on any of these men right now."

"You should take a chance," Elliott said to her.

"Oh yeah, says the man who won't let me introduce him to Kiana."

"That's different. You want to have someone pick at my brain and my thoughts and analyze me. What fun is that?"

"It will help you so that you can have a relationship maybe one day with a woman, although I don't know who would put up with your crap," she teased, and he chuckled but then pulled her into his arms and hugged her. She hugged Elliott tightly.

"I love you. You're the best," he said to her.

"And I love you, too." She pulled back.

He squinted at her. "So, you'll take a chance on Jordan and his brothers?"

"You'll meet Kiana and talk?" she countered.

Ben and Phoenix laughed. "Sounds like we're back to square one," Ben said. They walked her to her car, hugged her goodnight, and then watched her drive off.

When Melise got to her condo, she headed upstairs and thought about tonight and about Elliott's suggestion, but as she rounded the corner, she stopped short. There was Jordan, and he didn't look happy.

"What are you doing here?" she asked him.

"Unlock the door and let's go inside."

"What? No, I'm not letting you inside of my apartment. You followed me to the bar and now here. That's creepy."

"I wasn't the only one, now open the damn door," he said fiercely as his cell phone rang. She reached for the knob and unlocked it, and they went inside.

"Yeah, a black sedan, it's parked by the corner, one guy driving. He picked up on her at work and has been following since. ... Didn't recognize him, but I'm assuming he was hired by those assholes. ... Yeah, she's fine, I have her here. We'll wait for you to handle that." He ended the call and she stood there, arms crossed, and stared at him.

"I don't stalk women," he said as he glanced around the place. She raised both eyebrows up at him. "What? I don't."

"Oh really? How about the pier while I was painting?" she asked.

"Seriously? That was different."

"I don't see it that way, and it seems like you stalking me is becoming a regular occurrence. Bet you shocked yourself when you met your old military buddy at the bar and found out he's my brother."

He stepped closer and held her gaze. "It was a shock, but it also gave me relief."

"Relief?"

He closed the space between them, and she uncrossed her arms and let them fall to her sides. He gently touched the material of her dress on her hip and stared down into her eyes. "To know they were related, and not lovers." He pulled her snug against him, slid one arm around her waist and the other up under her hair and head. "I should have kissed you last night, but if I did, you would have come home with us, and we would still be in bed." He pressed his lips to hers as she processed his words and absorbed his kiss. He plunged his tongue into her mouth and was walking her backward until her back hit the wall by the door. She moaned into his mouth and felt his fingers slid up under her dress against her thigh. She felt so much, wanted so much in that moment, and it was wild. She shouldn't be doing this with him, yet she wanted to.

She pressed her palm against his chest, and then he lifted her up with one strong arm and hand, his fingers at her ass. He slid a digit along her crack over her thong panties, and she moaned deeper. She wanted those fingers closer to her cunt. Hell, inside of her cunt. In that moment, he found her pussy and pressed up into her. She gasped, pulled from his mouth, tilted her head back, and moaned.

"You're so wet, so fucking responsive. You want this. Want my brothers and me to pleasure you, hell, to fuck you," he said, and pressed his mouth to her neck as his fingers thrust and stroked into her cunt. She felt so much, too much. His mouth and chin maneuvered against the cleavage of her breast to try and take a taste. He couldn't, but she wanted him to, and she slid her hand up to her top and undid the buttons. He growled. "Holy fuck. I thought I would never feel again, Melise.

Where the fuck did you come from?" he asked, and then licked into the cup of her bra and found her nipple.

"Oh Jordan, oh God, this is wild."

"Incredible," he said. When someone knocked on the door, she squeaked aloud.

"Unlock it. Let them in," he said with his fingers still stroking her cunt.

"Jordan?" she said and held his gaze.

"They want you, too. Want this with you. Now, open the fucking door or they will break it down with worry," he said, and she reached down and unlocked it as he slid a finger over her asshole, lubricating it with her cream, and pressed a digit up into her.

"Oh!" she cried out very loudly as Pelham, Carson, and Warren entered the condo, closed the door, and started making comments.

"What is going on in here?" Pelham asked, and he caressed her hair from her cheek. Jordan pulled the finger from her ass and pressed another digit to her cunt.

"She's wet and very responsive, but naughty. She didn't even know someone was following her."

"You were," she said and gasped for breath.

"Not me, the other guy." He pushed his fingers faster, deeper.

"Oh God, please. Please," she begged.

"Come for us," Jordan said to her.

She stared into Jordan's deep green eyes as he pumped his fingers and she cried out her release. He pressed his mouth to hers, kissed her tenderly as he pulled his fingers from her pussy. She wrapped her legs around his waist tight. He was so big, so thick and hard, and he carried her as if she were light as a feather. Right to her bedroom, right in front of her bed as he set her down and began to undress her. "Oh God."

"Slow and easy. I'm not stopping now. I need more, Melise. Please. It's been too long since I felt a God damn thing," he said to her as her dress fell to the floor.

She reached up and cupped his cheeks. "I have to be out of my mind," she said to him.

"God damn, you're so beautiful," Warren said, and she looked at him, at Carson and Pelham standing there watching them.

"You all want me?" she asked them.

"If you'll have us," Pelham said, and he stepped closer. Jordan eased her back, her body fully exposed to them. She wore panties and a bra that barely covered her full breasts. "Say yes," Pelham said to her as he cupped her cheek and gazed over her breasts, licked his lips, and then looked back into her eyes.

"Yes."

"Thank God," Warren said, and Pelham pressed his lips to hers. She tilted up toward him while Jordan slid his hand to her bra and unclipped it in the back. He somehow held her up and against him with Pelham's help as he cupped her cheeks and jaw and ravished her mouth. They eased her onto the bed and began to fully explore her, kissing her everywhere their lips could reach. Carson was on the bed, naked, and sliding her panties down with Pelham's help, but then Carson slid fingers to her cunt. It was outrageous having them all touch her like this.

"You are super fucking wet. I love that. Fucking love it. You're incredible," Carson said, then kissed her next as Pelham stood up and undressed alongside Jordan. Warren was now naked and between her legs, spreading her wide and exploring her cunt with Carson. A slide of Warren's tongue, and then dip into her cunt, had her wiggling and moaning.

"Easy, princess. Easy," Carson said to her in that deep voice of his. These men were older, and it came out in their touches, their words, their actions, too.

"On the pill?" Pelham asked. She moaned as Warren thrust fingers in and out of her cunt. Carson suckled her breast, twirled his tongue over her nipple, and then nipped her skin.

"Oh God, I have an IUD, but if you guys have been active—oh!" She cried out another release.

"Let me in there," Jordan said to his brothers. To Melise, he said, "We're good. It's been a long time, baby. A long fucking time."

Warren pulled his fingers from her cunt, Carson released her breast, and Jordan slid his palms up and down her thighs and pulled her toward the edge of the bed. He locked gazes with her. "You're so damn beautiful. So fucking sexy. Look at this body. My God, I don't deserve you," he said and pressed his cock to her pussy.

"You do deserve me, and I deserve you. I need you, Jordan," she said to him. He pushed his thick, hard cock up into her cunt, and she moaned and gasped for breath. She absorbed the sight and feel of his body. The ripped abs, the tattoos, and, of course, the scars along his chest. She ran her hands up against them, and he grabbed her wrists and pressed her arms above her head. She gasped while he hammered into her. "Jordan!" she screamed, and he clenched his teeth and kept thrusting faster and faster, and then roared as he came. He fell slightly against her, suckled and breathed heavy against the crook of her neck, and she hugged him back, ran her hands through his hair, and tightened her legs against his waist.

He lifted up, looked at her, brought his hand to her cheek, and stroked her jaw. "I didn't hurt you, did I?"

"No. It was incredible," she said to him, and he swallowed hard.

"It was incredible to watch," Carson said, and they both glanced at him as he stood there stroking his cock, his thick, hard, muscular chest arousing her once again.

"Ready for me?" Carson asked.

"Ready," she said, and Jordan kissed her again before he eased up and Carson took his place.

* * * *

Carson didn't know what happened to bring this all on tonight, but he was thrilled. They were all attracted to Melise, kept talking about her and the deep desire to protect her and possess her, yet the fact that Jordan hadn't kissed her like they did made it feel like they couldn't make a move. Seeing them like they were tonight, the desire, the arousal strong and wild, he knew in that moment she was going to be theirs. His heart pounded inside of his chest.

He slid his palms along her hips and spread her thighs wider.

"Let me take a look at you. My God, you're perfect, Melise. Fucking perfect." He looked at Pelham and Warren, who were right there on the bed watching and stroking her skin.

"She's perfection. Look at these right here. I think they need some attention," he said while cupping her breasts. Her lips parted, and she moaned but held his gaze. Then Pelham and Warren leaned in, slid their palms to her breasts, and began to feast on her breasts. The sight had him nearly coming already.

"Holy fuck, she's ours. Ours," he said, slid his cock into her pussy, and thrust right into her. Melise gasped and held onto Pelham and Warren's heads while they suckled her breasts, as Carson thrust into her over and over again. He felt desperate, wild with desire to fuck and claim her. "No other men, Melise. No other men or I'll fucking lose it. You got it, baby? Just us now. Just us," he said, thrusting and stroking into her.

"Yes, Carson. Yes, oh God, please, I'm there, I'm—" She cried out and Carson followed, grunting and then cursing as he stroked into her a few more times.

"Holy God, baby. Fuck, I'm dizzy," he said, and Jordan placed his hand on his shoulder.

"She packs one hell of a punch," he said as Warren and Pelham released her breasts and Carson moved off the bed.

Warren slid between her legs, pressed her arms above her head, and then thrust right into her. "Mine," he said, and suckled against her neck, then slid his hands down from her wrists to her forearms and elbows as he thrust and stroked faster and faster.

"You're so wild, Warren. Oh God, yes, yes," she said to him, feeding Warren's ego. Jordan and Carson smirked, but Pelham looked wild and needy.

* * * *

Warren couldn't get enough of Melise. Of her sexy body, her lush curves, her big breasts, and those gorgeous green eyes of hers. She was a damn goddess and then some. How the fuck did they get so lucky? There was no way this was a one night stand, a temporary thing. No fucking way. With every thrust, he felt more and more. Then the feel of her hands on him, her fingers pinching his nipple, made him feel wild and naughty. Like he wanted to fuck every inch of her and mark her his woman. He pulled out, and she gasped as he flipped her onto her belly, slid her to the edge of the bed, stood up behind her, and thrust into her cunt from behind.

"Warren!" she cried out

He thrust and thrust, grabbed her round sexy ass and squeezed it, massaged the globes, and looked at her asshole. "Fuck, we're going to fill you up one day, baby. Fill every hole with cock and claim you as our woman together. You want that, Melise? Want a cock in your pussy, mouth, and asshole at the same fucking time? Huh?" he asked and thrust again and again.

"Oh!" she screamed out and came like a faucet. The sloshing sound filled the room, and he lost control. He came with a roar.

* * * *

Pelham watched Warren kiss every inch of Melise's skin before he eased from her pussy. Pelham took his place, lay over her, letting his thick, long cock smooth along her ass and her back. He slid her hair off her shoulders and kissed her cheek. She was breathing rapidly.

"You have the sexiest body, woman, and it's ours," he said and suckled on her neck a little harder. She moaned and then rocked her hips. "You ready for me?"

"Yes, Pelham. Oh God, this is crazy," she said, and he lifted her hips and aligned his cock with her pussy from behind and then slowly slid into her cunt. He massaged her ass cheeks, ran his palms up and down her back as she moaned and rocked her hips.

"Feel good?"

"Yes," she hissed.

"Need more?" he asked.

"Yes, faster, Pelham, please," she said. He began to move faster. Her pussy was leaking so much cream, he eased a finger under her and brought a wet digit to her asshole and began to explore her there.

"Pelham." She rocked her hips up and down.

"God damn, that is hot," Warren said, joining them on the bed. Carson and Jordan were there, too.

"She's ours. This cunt, this asshole," Pelham said and slid his finger into her asshole.

"Pelham! Oh, it burns."

"You'll get used to it, baby," Carson said, cupping her cheeks, tilting her head to the side so he could kiss her.

"Let him in, baby. Get a feel for it," Warren told her.

"Oh. Oh, yeah," she said and rocked her hips against Pelham's finger and cock.

"You are tight and wet back here. Your ass is begging for cock, woman."

"Oh please. Please," she begged, and he pulled out of her cunt.

He leaned over her and whispered into her ear, "You want me to fuck this ass, baby? You need it there?"

"I've never done that."

"That's perfect. We'll be the first and the only."

Smack.

Smack.

She gasped as he spanked her ass.

"Do it," Jordan said as he lay on the bed and slid fingers underneath her to her cunt. He stroked her. She widened her thighs.

"Just like that. More? Yes?" Pelham asked her.

"Yes," she said and rocked her hips. Her eyes were closed, and she was coming.

Pelham looked at Carson and Warren, then Jordan.

"No turning back," he whispered.

"Don't ever want to," Jordan said.

"In for the haul," Carson said.

"Our angel," Warren said.

Pelham felt his heart racing. He knew what this would mean, taking her in every hole and being the first men to do that. He eased his wet fingers in and out of her asshole. She rocked her hips and thrust her pussy down over Jordan's fingers. "So wet, so giving and ready."

"More," she moaned.

He pulled his fingers from her asshole and replaced them with his cock. As he breached her asshole and pushed into her, she moaned and shook, and he grunted and cursed. "So fucking tight. Oh God, baby. Oh God," he said and pushed all the way in.

"Oh!" she moaned loudly.

"I want in. Now," Jordan said, and Pelham wrapped one arm around her waist while Warren disappeared to the bathroom. Pelham lifted her up, Jordan lay back down, and he cupped her cheeks. "Ride me while my brother fucks that sexy ass," he said, and Pelham heard her moan and then felt the tightness as he and Jordan made love to her together.

"I can't believe I'm doing this. Oh, it feels so strange and yet so good," she said and exhaled as they slowly stroked into her cunt and asshole.

"Here I am," Warren said and climbed up on the bed. He cupped her cheek. "I want to feel your mouth on me. Like this together. All of us." She lifted her mouth toward his cock and began to suck Warren down.

"Holy hell. Look at you," Carson said, sliding his palm up and down her back and along her ass. She moaned against Warren's cock.

"Faster. Pick up speed, I'm already fucking there," Pelham said, and he thrust and thrust as Jordan stroked upward, and then Pelham came. He pulled out, and Carson took his place.

He made sure she was still wet and he slid his cock into her asshole. "Holy fuck, she's super tight. Jesus, how the fuck did you move, Pelham? Fuck." He grunted, held her hips, and rocked into her when Warren came in her mouth. "Holy hell."

"More Carson, Jordan. More. I feel something," she said, and the two of them thrust so hard, so fast but continued to make love to her until Melise came with a loud cry. Jordan and Carson followed, grunting, cursing, and then easing from her body and kissing her everywhere their mouths could reach.

"Holy shit," Carson said and fell to the bed. Pelham stumbled to the seat by the bed, and Jordan laughed as he hugged her against his chest and caressed her as she rested.

"Ours. Always," Jordan said, and his brothers all mumbled in agreement. Pelham smiled.

Chapter 5

Melise awoke feeling the warmth of two thick male bodies against hers. One hand was over her neck and shoulder, her mouth against Jordan's skin, and another hand was over her belly, fingers nearly to her pussy. These men were awfully possessive or seemed to be in sleep. She wondered how they would react this morning, and if Jordan would put up those walls of his. If Pelham would be all business, and maybe Warren would be ready to do it all over again, and Carson, too. It was Warren's fingers that were nearly to her cunt right now, and considering how many times they made love last night, she couldn't believe she was ready for them again. She started to lift back when Jordan's possessive hold of her tightened a little. "Rest a little longer," he said, voice hoarse and sexy.

Warren slid his fingers to her pussy. "Stay in bed with us where you belong," he whispered. Oh boy, were they commanding. His fingers pushed deeper. He lifted slightly and kissed her shoulder as she eased to her back. Jordan tilted her chin up and pressed his mouth to hers as Warren lifted higher so he could stroke her better. "Keep those legs wide open," Warren commanded, but then the bed dipped, another set of hands slid up her ankles and to her thighs.

"Good morning, gorgeous," Carson said. Jordan released her lips as Warren pulled his fingers from her cunt, and Carson stroked her there. She looked at him, head tilted back, trying to catch her breath and deal with the whole tag team thing. When she looked to see where Pelham was and didn't see him, she must have looked panicked.

"He's on the phone in the other room. Don't worry, we'll keep you occupied and wet for him," Carson said, then climbed higher to align his cock with her pussy. He gripped her hips while Jordan and Warren took her hands and raised them to the headboard. "Let go, give us all of you. No holding back," Carson said to her, and he pushed his cock into her cunt, and she accepted the invasion, despite feeling a bit sore.

"You're so big. God, how can you feel even bigger than last night?" she asked, shaking as he thrust into her pussy. The three of them chuckled.

"You were wild last night, begging for us to keep filling you up over and over again. You belong to us, baby. To all of us now," Carson told her, and she cried out as her orgasm hit her.

Pelham entered the room just as Carson came with a roar. Carson cupped her cheeks and kissed her lips then along each breast as he eased his cock from her body.

She caught sight of Pelham and locked gazes with him. "I'm not going to get any work done today, am I, Melise?" he asked in a reparatory tone, but then Warren lifted her up into his arms and kissed her as he adjusted himself to the edge of the bed. She lowered right down over his cock, knowing, anticipating what would come soon enough. Three cocks inside of her, three men claiming her body, marking her their woman. Warren slid his palms along her ass and widened her thighs as she rocked over him.

"Nice and wide. You know Jordan has a big dick, even bigger when he looks at this body of yours and wants in," Warren told her before he pulled her down to kiss him. She did and that was when she felt Jordan move in behind her and lick her asshole, then spread cream from her pussy over it. She felt his finger slide in, but she kept kissing Warren and countering his thrusts.

"Nice and wet," Jordan said, using his palms to spread her ass cheeks wider, and then moved them up and down her back, to her shoulders. He kept one hand on her shoulder as he pulled his finger from her ass and replaced it with his cock.

"Here I come," he said, and she felt the tip against the puckered hole, and a second later he thrust his cock into her asshole and all three of them moaned. Jordan gripped her upper shoulder as he rocked into her asshole from behind. Underneath her, Warren tilted up and down, fucking her in sync to his brother's strokes. She was panting and moaning, could feel her asshole and her pussy react to the dual penetration when a hand slapped her ass.

Smack.

She lifted her head and there was Pelham, cock in fist, using his other hand to caress her ass, to squeeze it, and then he gripped her hair and brought her mouth to his cock. He looked fierce, wild, and she thought for a moment that something was bothering him, but she couldn't ask. Wouldn't ask right now, instead focusing on the task at hand. Sucking his cock and making all of them one unit making love.

She bobbed her head up and down.

"That's right, baby, suck me good and deep. Claim me as your man like you did last night. Like you'll do whatever we ask or need you to."

Oh Jesus, his words were possessive and commanding. What did he expect? That she would follow him, them, around and let them fuck her whenever they wanted to? Her body yelled yes while she came again, apparently aroused by his words and actions, but her mind was worried. Then Jordan, obviously aroused at the idea, came in her ass.

"Fuck yeah," Warren said, and thrust again and again as Jordan pulled out.

"Release me," Pelham said, and she opened her mouth and Warren grunted and came. She was trying to catch her breath when Pelham got up, wrapped his arm around her waist, and pulled her lower to the edge of the bed. He placed her on all fours and then gripped her shoulder, slid his cock to her cunt, and thrust into her. He was relentless, stroking over and over again as she panted for breath and his brothers watched.

"Fuck her good, Pelham. Claim that pussy and then her ass. Make her see she belongs to us only and always," Carson egged him on, and Pelham stroked faster and deeper into her cunt. She was in awe of his stamina and the thickness of his cock. It was outrageous.

Over and over he thrust into her, and then he moved his hand from her shoulder and pressed a finger to her ass. She was so damn wet, her thighs sticky from her cum, and when he pulled out of her cunt and then pressed his cock to her asshole, she held her breath. He eased the thick, hard muscle into her ass, and they both moaned. She felt his body press over her, his mouth against her neck, sucking, biting her skin, then along her ear.

"You belong to us now. We'll take care of you and protect you, always," he said, and then thrust into her ass three more times before he paused to cup her breast. He suckled against her neck and give little bursts of thrusts into her asshole.

"Please, Pelham. I need more. Go faster, please," she said, and he eased fingers under her belly to her cunt.

"Oh," she gasped, and then he was relentless in his strokes. Over and over again he thrust into her ass, she cried out another release and panted for a break, for a second to try and keep up, but this was beyond anything she ever felt before. He rubbed her cream over her clit and pussy, applying pressure there as he slid in and out of her ass. The possessive hold he had on her, the way he dominated her body, and her position, fed her orgasm, bringing it closer and closer to surface. Her head spun, and then she closed her eyes and let go. She cried out his name. "Pelham!" and he grunted hers as he came in her ass, then shook as they came down from their high of making love again in bed.

* * * *

Jordan was putting his shirt back on after he took a shower. They were taking turns, Pelham and Warren were finished, he went before Melise, who was in the shower now. He inhaled and shook his head. They all smelled like her now. Like her shampoo, her soap, the fabric softener in her towels, even her perfume somehow. It annoyed him the instant he inhaled and liked smelling like her the first time he showered during the night. Then he accepted liking it and didn't say a word, but as he put the shirt on and inhaled, his brother Carson pointed it out, too.

"We all smell like Melise. Don't know how I'm going to concentrate on anything but her body and making love to her again," Carson complained.

"Take a shower at home later," Pelham said. He was definitely still in a bad mood.

"What's up? You've been pissed since early this morning."

One look at Warren and Carson, and Jordan knew it was something worrisome.

"The guy who was tailing her was not one of Masterson's guys but one of Merser and Dolinth's," Pelham told him.

Jordan clenched his teeth. "They'll go after her or use her to threaten us."

"That's what we're thinking, but this guy told our people that he reports to Masterson and Merser. Merser put Masterson and his guys in charge of this. The guy said she's important to them," Pelham explained.

"What the fuck does that mean?" Jordan asked.

"Well, she's not fucking ever going to be alone with any of them again. She goes to work and shouldn't have to meet with them at all, but if she does, then she does it with other people around," Carson said.

"Fuck that. She doesn't need to work at all," Warren stated.

"Yeah, that's going to fly?" Pelham asked.

"It will have to fucking fly. We've seen what those men can do to people they want to hurt, never mind muscle," Jordan stated.

"We aren't bending to them. We can't call and make any accusations, or it will make matters worse and show how much she means to us."

"Pelham, they know, and they'll figure out pretty damn fast that we're fucking her," Jordan raised his voice and started to pace. When he turned toward the doorway to the hall, there stood Melise, a shocked, hurt expression on her face.

"Fucking me?" she asked him.

"It isn't what I meant."

"You said it, that means you meant it," she retorted, then turned around and walked back to the bedroom.

He looked at his brothers. "Well?"

"We have to protect her. She's a bigger target as our woman," Pelham said.

"A lesser one as an interest," Warren whispered, then swallowed hard and ran his hand along his jaw, appearing like he felt like a dick for saying that and having to pretend last night meant less than it actually did.

"I'm not pretending shit," Jordan said.

"Jordan, behind closed doors, it will be like last night and this morning, but out there, we have to keep our distance," Carson said to him.

"We explain that how?" Jordan asked.

"By telling her our relationship needs to remain a secret while we deal with Merser, Dolinth, and Masterson," Pelham said and, then headed toward the bedroom.

* * * *

Melise started to put her hair up and anticipated a change of plans. Instead of spending more time with the men, she was being dismissed, and now had the rest of the day free. She felt like a fool. Like a woman who fell into a heat-of-the-moment decision, let down her guard as they requested, and allowed them full access to her body. She let them make love to her together. No, wait, fuck her together. Tears stung her eyes, and she heard the floor creak as she finished her hair and then adjusted her tank top and light beige skirt she wore.

"We need to talk," Pelham said. Those dark green eyes and that hardcore, seasoned expression that turned her on now annoyed her. She wanted to hate him, but truth was, she loved him. She loved all of them, and nothing ever felt so right and so perfect. Apparently, she was the only one who felt that way.

"Nothing to talk about," she said and started to walk toward her closet for her sandals. He grabbed her arm and pulled her toward him.

He towered over her, and she couldn't help but to be intimidated by him.

"Sit," he said and placed his hands on his hips.

She slowly sat on the edge of the bed.

"The guy who was following you was working for Merser and Dolinth." She squinted. "We explained a little about the work they're involved in and our positions."

"You make them pay money for use of establishing a storefront and selling illegal products," she said to him.

"Who told you that?" he asked. She narrowed her eyes at him. "Who told you that?" he repeated, and she knew he meant business.

"Masterson. He said you were bullies. That he was being forced to pay to have a storefront in your and Costanza's territory."

He licked his lower lip. "When did he have this conversation with you?"

"Yesterday."

He was breathing through his nostrils. "What else did he say in that conversation?"

"Things," she said, thinking about how he said the Marquis brothers fuck women and leave them. They don't do commitments, and they will hurt her.

"Melise, these men cannot be trusted."

"Neither can all of you, apparently."

She went to stand up, but he stepped forward and she fell back against the bed. He stared down at her as she leaned on her elbows.

"Last night, we made love to you together."

"You fucked me," she said and went to get up, but he gripped her thighs, causing her to fall to her back as he laid over her. He slid his palms up her body to her cheeks and cupped them.

Pelham held her gaze. "We made love to you, we didn't fuck you. We're hard men. Men who are involved in shit that we will not talk to you about or divulge to you, and as our woman, you must accept that. There'll be rules, Melise. You have to abide by our rules."

She swallowed hard and felt angry at herself for being turned on by his possessive hold on her, his dominant actions and words. What was wrong with her? "So one of the rules is to hide this…this affair."

He kept one palm against her cheek and the other he slid down under her skirt, against her skin to her hip. "We are not having an affair. We want you in our lives. We don't date, never have, but we will with you. Those men are up to something, and until we can figure out their next move, you are to abide by these rules."

"And not see you? Not touch you or kiss you in public? Is that what you mean? A relationship behind closed doors?"

"For now." He stroked her jaw with his thumb and tilted her chin upward.

"I want you," he continued. "My brothers want you every second of every minute. We would get lost in your body, in your presence, in your sexy, stunning eyes. We've never felt this way before, and it's bad fucking timing because of your job, Masterson being a client, and also being involved with bad men like Merser and Dolinth." He gripped her hip and gave her a little shake. "Please, baby, do not disobey my orders. Do as I say, as we all say, and keep this relationship hidden while we handle the other shit."

She wanted to believe him. He was expressing himself, and that was different in itself. "I don't like it," she said.

He gripped her chin and kissed her lips. He spoke against them. "I don't fucking like it, either, but risking your life or letting you get hurt because we weren't thinking with the right heads, I can't accept."

"Okay, Pelham."

He kissed her again, then stood up and pulled her up into his arms. "Let's make some plans," he said and walked her out of the room, holding her hand.

She looked at Carson and Warren first. Then at Jordan. "We all good?" Warren asked Pelham.

"Melise is on the same page as the rest of us," he said, and then Pelham's phone rang.

* * * *

Pelham didn't like this idea of not seeing Melise and making their relationship known, but it was Costanza's suggestion, because something else was brewing with the arrangement Merser and Dolinth had with Masterson, Cader, and Sal. They caught wind of another investor, and there was some sort of a connection to Wayworth Industries. Instead of pushing to get their cut from Merser and Dolinth, they needed to find out who else was involved with these illegal storage facilities, and what else was being shipped in and out through them.

"Hello?" Pelham answered the phone and walked toward the kitchen.

"Three accounts that Wayworth Industries have are owned by the same person but listed under three different corporations. I'm trying to dig deeper but don't want to draw any red flags. Can you guys take over from here?" Costanza asked.

"Definitely. We're getting ready to leave Melise's place, just going over a few rules," he said, looking toward the living room where Melise stood with his brothers. They were talking to her, and she was nodding her head.

"Be careful, and remember what I said. Something is going on here that isn't adding up."

"I hear ya. We'll get on it within the hour."

Pelham ended the call and then made his way over to Melise to say good-bye. She would need to understand what was happening here and abide by the rules, because he wasn't taking a chance with her life. No way. She had become instantly important to them, and he knew he wanted her in their lives forever, not just one night.

Chapter 6

"Oh!" Camille screamed out as William thrust into her from behind while he smacked her ass. He grabbed her hair and pulled her from the edge of the bed toward Louis.

"Suck his cock. Make up for being the dirty little whore you are, Camille," William reprimanded, making her body ache as he thrust again and again. She grabbed onto Louis's thighs and immediately took his cock into her mouth. William roared as he came. He smacked her ass a few times as he chuckled and pulled out of her. Now, Louis grabbed her hair, slid his cock from her mouth, and then pressed her body over the edge of the bed. He was balls deep in her cunt before she could take her next breath. Tears hit her eyes, but determination filled her soul. She was making money playing this game from all angles.

"Got things started without me, huh?" her other boss Gary asked, stepping out of his dress pants.

"How did the call go?" William asked him as he leaned back on one of the single chairs in the hotel room.

"The money was transferred to the accounts. Locust is thrilled. We got our cut," he said to them.

"Fuck yeah! And thanks to Camille's sexy, wet pussy, she got Masterson, Cader, and Sal on board, and they don't even realize how we'll be using their account, as well."

"I feel kind of badly for Melise. You think that bonus was enough?" William asked, and Camille felt her gut clench. After all she did for them, for the company, they were still hung up on that bitch.

"Well, you can always give her something else. A full paid vacation at a certain resort we all love," Louis teased.

"Yeah, that just so happens to be our place we own on the resort. Could you imagine being alone with her on a beach, no one from miles, that sexy body of hers in a string bikini?" William added.

"Fuck, the thought of her makes me want to—" Louis roared as he came in Camille's pussy. He pulled out and gave her ass a slap. As he walked away from her, leaving her there just laying over the bed, he enjoyed the conversation with Gary and William. She started to get up, but Gary was in a chair, naked and sipping a glass of expensive bourbon.

"Camille," he ordered and still looked at William and Louis as they discussed Melise's body, her ass, and how Masterson, Cader, and Sal were pursuing her, too. She went closer and he spread his thighs, indicating for her to give him a blow job. She was getting angrier and angrier. She figured after helping to secure the deal with Masterson over the contract with Wayworth Industries, then fucking Masterson, Cader, and Sal before helping them to get closer to Melise, while simultaneously launder money through all their companies with Locust Fender, the least these dicks could do was show her their full attention. Instead, they were discussing Melise and fucking her.

"Hey!" Gary grabbed her hair and yanked her up. "What the fuck, Camille?" he said, and she realized she had been too rough and nipped him. She slid her palms up and down his thighs.

"Where's my cut in all of this?" she asked him, knowing she was playing them, too, and would be very rich in the next few days and then out of here.

"You'll get it. You aren't going anywhere, and neither are we. Got a lead on another potential client. We'll need your"—he looked over her breasts and then pinched her nipple—"special techniques to seal the deal."

"Why not ask Melise, since you three like her so much?" she asked and pulled away from him, but as she turned, Gary grabbed her by her arm and had her over his lap.

"Don't be jealous, Camille. Melise is a bit younger. Give her time, and maybe she'll become just as useful to this operation as you have become."

Louis and William chuckled, and Camille saw red, but she couldn't do anything about it now. She made her bed. So as Gary turned her around and pressed her to the floor on all fours, she bit her tongue and let him have his way with her. It would all be worth it, unless Merser and Dolinth, Masterson, Cader, and Sal found out they were getting duped out of money.

* * * *

Melise was painting on the pier Sunday, wondering if she would hear from Pelham and his brothers. Something went down this morning, and they didn't give her details but promised her that this situation would all be over soon. She wanted to believe them, especially as she sat here on the pier, under her umbrella and painting the storefronts. It led to a scene of couples holding hands, spending time together, and even ménage relationships, too, which seemed to stand out even more to her today than ever before. Was she stupid to think that something could actually come out of more than twenty-four hours of great sex with four powerful men?

It wasn't feeling too promising.

"Hey, gorgeous," she heard the familiar voice and covered her eyes as she turned and spotted her brothers. Elliott was walking between them, and he had sunglasses on and a hat.

"What are you guys doing down here today?" she asked, standing up to hug them hello, but Elliott seemed tense. "Elliott, are you okay?" she asked him.

"Fine," he said, and then looked at her painting. "That looks great."

"Thanks," she said and sat down.

"How long have you been out here?" Ben asked.

"Four hours."

"Shouldn't you be more along than that?" Elliott asked, knowing that when she was into her paintings, she would paint constantly and could finish a scene rather quickly. She shrugged her shoulders.

"Guy trouble?" Phoenix asked.

Phoenix and Elliott stood by the railing, and Ben took a seat on the bench.

"It's a long story."

"Is it why you didn't answer your phone Saturday night or this morning?" Phoenix pushed.

"So, I took a chance. It's complicated." She looked away.

"Did they hurt you?" Elliott asked.

She looked at him. "No, but there were some other things I hadn't mentioned to you, and they're in the way of progress."

"Okay, let's hear it," Ben said.

She chuckled. "Maybe I don't want to share it right now."

"Tough shit. Do it," Elliott said.

"I took the chance, so if I tell you guys everything, are you going to let me call Kiana so you can meet her?"

"Fine," he said. She pulled out her cell phone. "What are you doing?"

"Letting her know you agreed and that we're here at the pier. Sometimes she's either running or reading on the beach on Sundays."

Elliott looked that way and then exhaled.

"You'll be fine, and we'll be right here. It will be good for you, Elliott. Maybe help make the episodes less and less until they don't exist anymore," Ben added.

"We'll see."

As Melise explained what happened, her brothers were more concerned.

"All of these men are interested in you or perhaps trying something on you to get to Jordan and his brothers to stop them from getting the cut the Lopez and Marquis men are entitled to?" Phoenix asked.

"Initially that's what they believed, which was sort of stupid on Masterson's part, and even Merser and Dolinth because of how powerful both families are. Pelham and his brothers are working on something now. Some new information or something. I don't know, and that's part of the rules of being involved in a relationship with men like them, I guess."

"You seem untrusting and sad," Phoenix said to her.

She explained about the conversation she overheard and Jordan's words, but then about Pelham.

"Jordan is stubborn like I am," Elliott said. "Plus, add in the PTSD and not liking to be social, and he'll be the last one to fully show any kind of vulnerability, but he cares about you. I saw it in his eyes at the bar that night."

"We talked about it, and I understood what Jordan meant, it just hurt to think that they would minimize what we shared. I've heard some horror stories with guys who made women believe they wanted to share her and be in a committed relationship, and they didn't. I just don't want to be taken advantage of. Then add in the work stuff, and I don't know. It makes me uneasy."

"That's expected. When are you going to see them again?"

"Whenever they call and say they can."

She saw Phoenix's eyes and Jordan's eyes look at something behind her, and then Ben turned. They were all in a dead stare, and when she turned around to look, there stood Kiana.

"Kiana," Melise exclaimed and got up and gave her friend a kiss hello. Kiana was gorgeous, with brown hair and emerald green eyes. She was petite and sexy, very toned, and loved working out. She wore a cover-up in white, and it showed off her tanned skin.

"Meet my brothers," Melise said, and as she introduced them, her brothers ate up Kiana with their eyes, and she couldn't help but smile. Was that how she looked when she saw Jordan? How Jordan looked, staring at her? She wondered and then laughed as it seemed Kiana found them just as attractive, as well.

* * * *

"Carson." Melise gasped as he lifted her t-shirt up over her head and tossed it. He shoved down her shorts and panties, and then lifted her up and carried her to the bedroom. Warren was in tow, but not Pelham and Jordan. He dropped her onto the bed, yanked off his clothes, and then covered her body with his. He plunged his tongue into her mouth and ravished her as Warren undressed and dropped something onto the bed.

"I need you so badly. I fucking missed you. Missed being inside of you," Carson told her as he cupped her cheeks.

"I missed you, too. I hated it," she admitted.

"Well, we're here now, and we're going to take you together." He tapped a tube of lube against his hand, and her body shivered with desire.

"I need that," she said.

"Good," Carson said, and then lifted her up. He turned around and fell back onto the bed with her straddling his hips. "Show us how much you missed us, too."

She caressed up and down his chest with her palms. She tugged on his nipples and bent lower to nip them. She felt his cock press against her belly, and then Warren was behind her.

"Nice and easy," he said, and Carson moaned.

"You're killing me," he said, and she eased down his body, kissing, suckling on him, and then licking his cock as Warren pressed the cool lube to her asshole. She paused.

"No, keep fucking going," Carson commanded. She did. She began to suck him as Warren slid fingers into her asshole. It felt different, not so much of an ache. Not that she minded. She had been so wet when they were all kissing her and stimulating her body. She begged for it, and right now she wanted that sensation again. She lifted up and gripped his cock. Holding Carson's gaze as he cupped her breasts and manipulated the nipples, she eased down over his shaft as Warren pumped faster behind her.

"Holy fuck, so tight and wet. You're heaven, baby. Your pussy is fucking heaven," he said, and she chuckled.

Warren gripped her hips. "Lower down, rock those hips and ride him. I can't hold back. I need this ass now," he said.

Smack.

She gasped but then began to ride Carson's cock, up and down, his thick, hard shaft hitting her womb and making her pussy tighten. Then Warren pulled his fingers from her ass and replaced them with his cock. He nudged and nudged and then thrust into her asshole, making the three of them moan.

"Oh please. Oh my God, yes, yes," she said, and both men started to thrust into her pussy and her asshole. She held on best she could, but then let go and cried out her release.

"It looks as good as it sounds," Pelham said as he and Jordan joined them.

Immediately, Jordan was on the bed, naked, cock in hand. He caressed her hair. "Missed you," he said.

"I missed you, too," she said before she took his cock into her mouth and began to suck him down.

"There. I'm fucking there," Warren yelled out and came. He caressed her back and her hips and her ass, then pulled out.

"Perfect timing," Pelham said, and eased right into position behind her, thrusting right into her asshole. They all moaned and rocked their hips, and then Carson came, Jordan followed, Melise was next, but Pelham kept going and going, and then thrust into her hard and came.

* * * *

Pelham held Melise on his lap after they made love several times and showered. The pizzas they brought over were cold, but they were all starving. He caressed her belly under the long t-shirt she wore, and it made him want her all over again. It was insane. He was obsessed with her.

"So, we have some questions for you," he said, and she looked at him with concern. "We're not sure you'll be able to answer the questions, but we hit a brick wall with our resources. We think we know what's going on but need proof."

"Okay," she said. He continued to stroke her belly under her shirt, and she pulled it down so her pussy wouldn't be exposed. He found that kind of cute that she would still be shy around them after all they'd done.

"Okay, so basically you understand what this situation is about between us, the Lopez brothers, and Merser and Dolinth, right?"

"They have a warehouse and storefront they own in your territory, and if they want to run a business they need to give you a cut?" she asked.

"Not just any business. We aren't corrupt gangsters. So regular retail stores, whatever, are fine. These particular men are using the storefronts and the warehouse facilities to filter through and store illegal merchandise and drugs."

Her mouth gaped open.

"Since we own the territory, if they want to do such things, then they need to pay up. Thing is, Merser and Dolinth are greedy fucks, and they've kept the business under wraps for a while, but recently they got more business, making a lot more money, and they're trying to push back to get a response. My brothers and I have done more legit business dealings for a while, some investments, and, well, being the muscle, the ones to send a message is not really our thing anymore. We'll do it if need be, but we're above that shit."

"So, since I wound up in the middle that night at the business dinner, they thought they could use it as an opportunity to challenge your power and perhaps threaten you?"

"No one threatens us," Jordan said to her. She sealed her lips.

"We have a lot of capabilities," Pelham continued, "and during our investigation we came across some information that could help relieve the situation and get everything back on track."

"What do you mean?"

"Someone is setting up accounts under false companies or attaching these accounts to current companies Wayworth Industries has established, and they're using those accounts to do something illegal."

"Like what?"

"Not sure. We've tracked the accounts set up by Masterson with your company, and so far there's only one account labeled international expenses."

"That can't be. Masterson's company and products are sold only in the United States. We don't even set that up in their account unless they're an international company."

Pelham looked at his brothers.

"Could definitely be the other option, then. That the owners of the company or someone within the company is creating additional accounts under the same legit company names and storing money there," Carson said.

"Money laundering?" she asked, and Pelham was surprised.

"You understand how that works?"

"Of course. When did you look up that account, and how did you get in?"

"Don't ask questions," Warren said to her.

"Okay. Well, if by chance someone is doing that, and they're using Masterson's company amongst others, then those accounts won't be there long. The company has a strict accounting procedure, and it's done every three months. That account can be wiped out, removed and no one would ever know it had been there," she said to them.

Pelham rubbed his jaw. "We need concrete evidence that we can approach Masterson with."

"Wait, what if the storefronts, the warehouse, those little buildings that are vacant right now, are all ways for Merser, Dolinth, and Masterson to launder money?"

"You think they're allowing Wayworth Industries to do it?"

"Could be if they get a cut. Although, when it comes to business like that, I don't think Masterson, Sal, and Cader are too smart with things. I think Merser and Dolinth control them."

"Shit, then we're back to square one," Carson said.

"No, you have information on them and can bring trouble their way," she said.

"As long as it brings that trouble away from you, I'm fine with that," Pelham said to her, and then eased his palm up over her breast, exposing her belly and pussy to him and his brothers.

"Pelham," she reprimanded and went to push her shirt down.

"Arms back," he said while holding her gaze. The woman was precious, gorgeous, and very sexy. She slowly raised them up and back, and he pushed her top to her neck. He ran his palm up and down her body, over her breasts. He played with her nipples and then slid a finger down between her thighs. She tilted her pelvis upward. "We want you safe and happy. The best place to have you to ensure that is with us, by our sides. We're concerned about you working at Wayworth Industries."

Her eyes widened. She tilted her head back and looked at Jordan, who was caressing her hair, then at Carson and Warren, who were sitting on the coffee table right across from her.

Pelham slid his fingers into her pussy. "We aren't asking you to quit your job, but you need to be aware and be smart."

Warren and Carson reached out and cupped her breasts, playing with her nipples, and then Carson leaned down and suckled her tit, tugging on it.

"Until we figure out what exactly is going on here, we'll be spending a lot of time with you out of work."

"I thought we needed to keep our…relationship, oh…a secret?" she said as she moaned while he thrust fingers faster and Carson nipped her tit.

"We missed you way too much, and letting those dicks know that you belong to us, to the Marquis family, will provide you protection, unless they have a death wish," Jordan said. She tilted back reached for him, and Jordan lowered his mouth to hers and kissed her.

When he released her lips, she smiled. "Just so you know, I feel it, too. I missed you so much, and I want you to know that I love you," she said to them.

Pelham felt so much. A deeper, more protective sensation instantly consumed him. "I love you, too," he said.

"As do I," Carson told her and tilted her chin up toward him, then he kissed her. When he released her lips, Warren cupped her breast.

"And I love you, sexy, and this body, and that sweet, wet cunt and sexy, fuckable ass," he said, and she shook her head at him and laughed.

She looked up at Jordan. He caressed her hair from her cheeks.

"I love you, Melise. From the first moment I laid eyes on you, I knew life would change. You made me feel again, made me smile again, and I will love you and protect you forever."

Pelham watched them kiss as he slid his fingers from her pussy, and she lifted up and Jordan pulled her into his arms. She fell on top of him on the couch.

"Looks like we're heading back to bed again," Warren said, clapping his hands and standing up. They snickered, but Pelham had an uneasy feeling, and he didn't like that sensation at all. It was one thing to worry about him and his brothers, but another to worry about a woman they loved. About Melise. If anyone tried to hurt her, he'd kill them.

Chapter 7

"Pull the accounts," Locust Fender said to Camille.

"What? No. I'm not pulling anything. We have these assholes by the balls."

"You did for a while and they are none the wiser, but now, I got the fucking Marquis men snooping through things. I don't understand how the fuck they're involved with this. They get their money from the territory Merser and Dolinth are using. That's how it goes. You're pulling money from using their property to launder more money and set up fake accounts at that firm of yours. Somehow, either the Marquis men figured it out, or someone else is fucking with the money and taking it. Either way, I want my name off of it. Having men like the Marquis and Lopez families on your ass means destruction. I've worked too fucking long, Camille."

Camille was in a panic. Those fucking men were destroying her entire operation. These men thought they could fuck her, bend her over a desk and have her do shit and think she wouldn't be able to figure out how to screw them? They were all going to suffer. Every fucking one of those scumbags. She needed another few days. A week would be perfect.

"I can't pull the accounts right now. I have three days left, then I can empty the accounts, cash out, destroy the accounts, and be done. Dolinth and Merser are resistant to the rules on their end for some stupid reason. That isn't our problem."

"What about your bosses? The greedy fucks have been setting up other accounts, yet they haven't paid me my share yet. They're a week late."

"Tell them to pay you."

"That's your job, Camille. Remember, I'm a silent partner in your operation. You needed the front money for your scam."

"Well, I paid that to you already."

"You did, but then you offered me a cut when you needed the computer software. Cut the job. It had a good run, but you're gaining attention for some fucking reason."

"I'll get the attention off of us. Just another week."

"No. I'm out. Get me my money tonight." Locust dismissed her, and she slammed her hand against the wall. All these fucking problems and it was going under, why? Because of fucking Melise. All those men wanted that bitch. What if Camille pinned shit on her? The international account was attached to Masterson's business file. She could send money into Melise's account at work. She still had passwords and could change anything she wanted. She could also take some of the bosses' profits from the money laundering and put it into Melise's account. Then, they would have to talk to her and do their thing. Maybe force themselves between her legs in the office and make her be their latest screw. It would take the pressure off of Camille, would send those Marquis men after the bosses. Masterson and them would want to go after Melise and the Marquis men, and Camille could take off with all the money.

Hmm. Complicated? Yes. Could it work? Maybe. Or was there an easier way to cause enough of a distraction that the Marquis men, Masterson, and her bosses would be too self-absorbed to even try to find Camille and the money she stole from all of them? Camille smiled. She had some planning to do.

* * * *

"So, when did this all happen?" Nina asked Melise over the phone as Melise finished up at work.

"Oh, like Costanza hasn't filled you in."

Nina chuckled. "I was told not to ask questions when it came to business associates, even those bedding my best friend."

"Bedding me, huh?" Melise asked and laughed.

"Do you have an escort there for you or what?"

"Not tonight. I'm heading right to the gym. Have my change of clothes and everything. I have to text them when I leave here, then when I get to the gym, and afterwards then when I get home." She chuckled.

"Very possessive. I love it. I don't really know them that well, but they seem dangerous, and I think they used to beat people up to get them to comply with rules. I don't know. I heard some small talk here and there."

"Well, they are very demanding, Possessive, yes. Dominant, yes. Actually, a lot like Costanza, Merdock, and Covaney are with you."

"It's so crazy, isn't it? Hey, I heard that Eduardo saw Antonia at a bar in Trenton, and she was talking to some guy, and Eduardo basically moved right in front of the guy, dismissing him."

"What? She didn't tell me that."

"When was the last time you spoke to her?"

"Hmm, you're right. Things have been crazy. We should get together."

"Will your lovers let you out of bed when you aren't working?" Nina teased.

"Sounds like a woman with experience," she countered, and Nina giggled. "Let's make plans."

"Well, something is going on right now. Merc and Fort are here with me. Mavis and the others are with Costanza, Merdock, and Covaney. They're having some sort of meeting or something. I think your men are there."

"I wonder what that's about."

"No, no, no, you aren't allowed to wonder, remember?"

"Melise?" Eleanor said her name, and Melise told Nina she would talk to her later about plans.

"Hey Eleanor, what's going on? I was just heading out."

Eleanor looked upset. Melise held her gaze.

"I hate to even ask this. It seems like something is wrong, but Mr. Wayworth just contacted me and asked that you go to his office immediately. He asked me if you had access to financial accounts of clients. Specifically four of them, Mr. Reynolds, the most recent."

"What? How could I have access to accounts? I submit any work I've done to accounting and billing, and they take care of fees. I don't allocate money at all. That isn't my job."

Eleanor squinted. "Something fishy is going on here," she said.

Melise thought about what her men had told her. She couldn't let Eleanor in on any of that, because it was illegal what they did to find out the information, but it seemed like someone in the firm was laundering money and using clients' accounts to do so.

"Well, you head up," Eleanor continued. "I'm going to do a little investigating. You know Camille had access to a lot of things. You basically got her fired. She could have sabotaged you or could still have access to things."

"Could she? I mean, you think she's behind this?"

"Maybe. It won't be that hard to track. I know I missed a few days of work being sick, but I can backtrack, and I'm very organized. You better head up. And don't let him intimidate you."

"Got it."

Melise was nervous as she exited the elevator. It was so quiet up there, and everyone had already left who worked on that floor. She passed the main desk, then Mr. Wayworth's personal assistant's desk, and even she was gone. Her gut clenched. She knocked on the door.

"Come in," he said, and she entered his office. "Close the door, Melise," he ordered, and she did.

"What's going on, Mr. Wayworth?"

He exhaled and stared at her. "That's why you're here. So we can figure it out. How long have you had access to the accounting system and financials?"

"I don't have access to them."

"Don't play dumb with me, Melise. This is serious shit here. My account has zero dollars in it. Several other accounts are missing a lot of money from them, and the clients are going to find out. They'll call the police, hell, the feds. Now, whatever reason you did it, fix it."

"I don't know what you're talking about. I wouldn't even begin to know how to do any of that and wouldn't have access to passwords and codes. Someone else must have done it."

"Then why the fuck does your account have five hundred thousand dollars in it?"

"What?" She jumped up from her seat.

"Look." He slightly turned his computer toward her, but she had to go behind his desk to get a clearer look.

She bent lower to see. "That's a mistake."

"No shit. We've got ourselves a problem, Melise. It shows your login code and password transferring money from four different accounts into your account. Did you think I wouldn't figure shit out?" he asked, and she felt him press up against her back. His arm went around her waist and his hand gripped her hair, tilting her head sideways. He suckled against her neck and rocked his hips against her ass. She could feel his erection.

"Let go of me. I didn't do this."

"You did. You and that cunt, Camille. She thought she had us fooled, but we took the money out of the accounts and faked the numbers. The money is gone. She doesn't have shit. Now there's only one thing to do, and that's call the cops and have you arrested and charged. Your career and life will be over."

"Oh God, please, I didn't do this. I don't know anything about Camille stealing, either."

He slid his hand up her belly to her breast and cupped it.

"Mr. Wayworth, get off of me." She clenched her teeth and threw her head back, hitting his nose. He released her, and she struck him in the face. "I'll have the cops arrest you for sexual harassment and assault."

"You bitch. I'll tell them you attacked me when I confronted you on this."

"I'll tell them you and your buddies are using fake accounts to launder money."

His eyes widened. "You won't do shit. We know people, and you're going to be our next fuck toy. Isn't that right, Gary?" She swung her head around to see Gary standing there, but Gary shook his head.

"Camille took all the money. It's gone. Those accounts are fake. She fucked us."

"What?" Mr. Wayworth yelled.

"I don't know what's going on, but I didn't do a thing wrong. Camille has been nothing but a problem. One you all created by allowing her access to accounts and passwords. She set other employees up and got them fired. It seems to me like she did the same thing to you. She went after your money and stole from you."

"That bitch," Wayworth yelled.

"Masterson called, too. Said that his bank called and money was withdrawn and placed into an account here."

She didn't stick around to hear the rest. She shoved by Gary and ran down the hallway to the elevator. She pulled out her cell phone and called Pelham but got no answer as it went to voicemail. She started to text when the elevator doors opened. Eleanor wasn't in sight, and Melise wasn't sticking around for more trouble. She grabbed her things and ran from the office building and went to her car, but as she went down the aisle her car was parked in, Cader was waiting for her. "Melise, we need to talk. Come with me now."

"No. I'm not going anywhere with you."

"Yes, you are." He grabbed her upper arm and pulled her with him. She screamed for him to release her, and then she heard the gunshot, and as she turned she was struck in the back of the head. She fell to the ground, the pain instant and through her head, now her neck and spine. Her vision blurred and then everything went black.

* * * *

"That bitch works for you?" Merser Volcheck yelled into his phone at Pelham.

"Who are you talking about?"

"Melise Minter. She stole from us. From Masterson, too, and when he sent Cader to pick her up from work, the bitch shot him and disappeared."

"That's bullshit. If you lay one fucking hand on her, Merser, I'll kill you," Pelham yelled into the phone. As Merser explained what he knew had happened, Pelham and the others began to come up with their own ideas.

"Melise is not the one who stole from you or from Masterson. We've been meeting trying to figure out what this side business was you have going that you aren't willing to pay us our share. We came across some discrepancies in accounts at Wayworth Industries," Pelham said as his brothers tried to get in touch with Melise. Costanza was sending guys to the office to question people and her bosses.

"We weren't doing anything that would take money from you or the Lopez family. We had our own thing going on the side. Next thing we know, we got nothing but problems. Someone took shit from their accounts, and money was taken from one of our accounts we had set up as a side company."

"You're laundering money, and you just got screwed, too. Whoever did all this fucked you all. It wasn't Melise."

"Then why did she shoot our guy?"

"Is he conscious or is he dead?"

"Conscious."

"He saw Melise shoot him?"

"No. He was holding her arm, she moved, the gunshot went off, and he fell back and hit his head."

"You call your men off of Melise. We'll get to the bottom of this," he said as he got into the SUV after they all exited the house.

"Got the guys at the office, they're grabbing the surveillance video coverage from outside. It's dark, but there was another person there.

They shot Cader, then struck Melise in the back of the head. She went down. The person was wearing all black. They pulled her out of there and out of the camera's view."

"Fuck. What else? I'm almost there with Costanza and them."

"A woman from Melise's office is here. Jordan has one of her bosses, who has a bloody nose, up against the wall."

"I'm here." He hung up.

As Pelham got to the upper floor and to Melise's bosses' offices the truth came out. He tried to attack Melise, and she headbutted him and then struck him. He then went on to explain about the money being stolen. His two partners, Louis and Gary, added their information, and then Eleanor came in.

"It was Camille. Camille did it all. She wiped out all the accounts. The four clients', and your three accounts. The transfer of the money in Melise's was just done a few minutes ago."

"Shit, she has access somehow. Any way to get a location on her?" Pelham asked.

"That's our area of expertise," Jordan said. "Eleanor, show me the system and the accounts."

Eleanor looked at Mr. Wayworth.

Jordan pressed the gun to his throat. "Don't look at this dick for approval. He assaulted our woman, caused this hit to happen, and now Melise has been abducted and is hurt. He'll approve anything we want so he doesn't go to jail and the feds don't learn about this. Unless, of course, something happens to Melise. Then, you're all fucking dead."

* * * *

Camille stared at Melise. She had to drag her ass to the boatyard and get her into the old office at the marina. Camille looked at the computer screen. She was filthy fucking rich, and those dicks lost a shit load of money. She would have loved to wipe them out entirely. Seen those smug expressions turn to shock. She thought she would have had more time. Then she saw the activity on the computer system and the accounts. Saw that Eleanor's password was used and she was going into the accounts. Camille knew the jig was up, she just hoped that Masterson got to Melise and killed her before he figured out it was Camille who screwed him. Then, as they killed Melise, Melise's boyfriends, those loser gangsters would have shot and killed Masterson, Cader, and Sal, maybe even Merser and Dolinth.

Well, her plan took a different turn. There was more money for her. She hadn't planned on killing Cader, but he showed up. No one would care if Cader died, plus no one would want that kind of thing happening to alert the police, either. It worked out. Camille could tell that Cader, Masterson, and Sal cared for Melise and didn't want to hurt her, so she had no choice. Now, she had to transfer the money to the off-shore accounts, then get rid of Melise.

This was going to take some time, but there was no hurry. No one could find them. Melise was out cold, and Camille would be on a cruise ship to the paradise by tomorrow morning.

She typed away on the computer, having set up an internet connection months ago. The rent she paid on this place was worth it. A small business office by the front entryway of an old marina. She smiled. This worked out perfectly.

Every so often, she glanced back at Melise, who was bleeding from her head. Her complexion didn't look good at all. Melise was white as a ghost, and her lips looked bluish. Perhaps she wouldn't have to kill her. Maybe Melise would just die right here. It wasn't like Camille needed to worry about the body or the blood.

She transferred the name of the lease into Wayworth's name and even had him sign documentation. That way if this place and all the files were found, the feds would look to him as the criminal. When Melise's dead body stunk up the place, William, Louis, and Gary would all be suspects, and she would be laying on a beach out of the country and filthy rich.

As she typed on the computer screen, she noticed how slow it was going. She slammed her hand down on the desk. "Not now. I need you to work. Come on," she said aloud and waited as the little ball swirled around, indicating it was trying to connect but it was taking too long.

She thought back to her time spent with William, Louis, and Gary. How she had been so stupid to believe that they wanted her for more than just sex? She made them need her. Need her body, her abilities, and her willingness to take risks. They truly believed that she loved them so much that she would take the fall if their money laundering operation was ever discovered. Dumb fucks. They looked at women as being stupid, clueless, and good for sex. Nothing more. Not her. No, she showed them. Now, they were fucking poor, and they would desperately have to hold onto the accounts they had and hope they got more. However, she also transferred money from accounting and there wouldn't be enough to pay taxes, pay the bills that would continue to pile up. Ultimately, they would fail, have to claim bankruptcy, and that put a smile on her face.

As she made the connection on the computer and began to pull up her account to transfer to the overseas accounts, she saw the number 0. "Zero? No, No, this isn't right," she yelled and started hitting buttons. She logged off and then logged back on. Someone fucked with the accounts. Someone stole everything from her, but who? Who knew what she had been up to? Who would be able to do this to her?

She jumped up and shoved the computer and all the things on the desk across it. They landed on the floor, things hitting Melise's body. She turned around and raged. She kicked Melise in the stomach and then in the face. She raged on her, blood now on her knuckles and fists when her mind refocused.

"Locust. You motherfucker. You're a dead man walking." She got up, yanked open the metal filing cabinet, and pulled out several guns. A semi-automatic, extra ammo, a Glock she placed into her jeans on the waist. Then she grabbed her keys. Camille glanced at Melise.

"Die, bitch. Die a painful and lonely death."

* * * *

Everyone was had their men out looking for Camille and her vehicle, but there was no such luck. Then Warren made a connection to phone calls Camille made to none other than Locust Fender.

"That scumbag. He's a loan shark. What the fuck was he doing talking to Camille?" Carson asked.

"Filtering stolen bills through the system. An easier way to clean them so nothing can be tracked," Jordan said as he rubbed his jaw. They had been at this for hours.

"Fuck, this is taking so damn long. Where the fuck is Locust anyway?" Covaney asked.

"Francesca is getting a hold of him," Costanza informed them.

It was taking hours, and every minute that passed their concern for Melise's life grew deeper. Where the fuck could Camille have taken her?

Pelham was losing his patience as no further information was coming in, and there hadn't been any word from Francesca.

"Well?" Pelham said to Carson and Warren.

"It's a weak signal, but we got a rough vicinity. I'm trying to pinpoint a closer proximity. It isn't easy. I can see the transactions, and I've withdrawn the money and moved it to another account," Warren replied.

"Jesus, the longer she's gone, the more that sick bitch could be doing to Melise," Jordan said.

Warren was typing faster, and he had two different screens going. Carson was there, too, typing away and highlighting lines of money and then clicking on the mouse and sliding them to another location.

"What are you doing now?" Pelham asked.

"Taking away what she stole and putting it elsewhere for now," Warren said.

"Won't that piss her off? Make her do something worse to Melise?" Jordan asked.

"With all that money, she can escape anywhere. We have to destroy any and all resources she has. Carson is working on pinpointing that signal. If we can get close enough to an area, we can start looking on foot."

"Jesus, I'm glad you guys are on our side," Costanza said, and Warren laughed, then clicked the button and sat back. The screen as rolling and then went to one line.

"There we go. Now she has nothing."

Pelham's cell phone rang. "It's Locust," he said to them, and they all stared at him.

"Locust, where's my woman?" he demanded to know.

"I don't have your woman. Didn't even know she was yours until I started getting these threats coming in through my sources. You know I would never fuck with your family or the Lopez family."

"Well, somehow with your little money laundering side business with that bitch, Camille, you did fuck with us. She took Melise. Knocked her out, and she could kill her next."

"Jesus, that bitch has lost her fucking mind."

"Where does she hide out? Where would she go?"

"I'm not sure."

"Hey, ask him if she would be anywhere near Fifth and Langley, and as far as the old abandoned boatyard. The one inland, nowhere near the water," Carson said to Pelham.

"Did you hear that?"

"Yeah. Hold up a second, let me ask one of the guys. He might know."

Pelham waited, breathing through his nostrils.

"He said maybe near the boatyard. Thought she rented some place there but not anymore."

"Fuck."

"We'll look anyway," Costanza said, and they all started to get up and plan teams to search for Camille and Melise.

"You fucking call me if you come up with something else, and Locust, you will pay for this," Pelham said and ended the call.

* * * *

Melise was moaning. Her head was throbbing so badly she couldn't even lift it off the floor. She couldn't move anything. Her face throbbed, her lips were swollen, and her stomach ached. What happened? Who beat her up and struck her over the head? Where was Cader? Was Masterson going to kill her because he thought she stole from him?

Tears poured from her eyes, but she cringed. Everything hurt more, even her head. She tried looking around, but as she moved her eyes the room spun. Her stomach lurched—she threw up and moaned in pain. She fell back to the floor, her cheek to the dirt, and she closed her eyes and wished the pain would go away.

* * * *

Camille was in a rage as she fired her weapon, taking out several of Locust's security guards. She was so angry, so filled with rage knowing that Locust tricked her and that he took all the money for herself that she didn't care what happened. She would die killing him if need be. As she rounded the corner and went to take more shots, someone came up from behind her and struck her down to the ground. Her gun was taken from her, and two men lifted her up, cuffed her hands behind her back as she flailed and kicked and screamed. They dragged her along the warehouse floors, and then Locust appeared, his cell phone to his ear and a gun in his hand.

"She's right here. She killed several of my men, and she will die for that," Locust said with the phone on speaker.

"Where is Melise?" She could hear a male voice.

"Fuck you," she replied. Locust nodded to two other men, and they struck her in the stomach and then the face several times. Each strike took her breath away, but anger was greater and getting some sort of revenge on Locust needed to be done.

"Find out where Melise is or you all die," the male voice said.

"Where is she, Camille? You live if you tell him. If you don't, he will kill everyone in his path," Locust told her.

"Too late. She looked dead when I left her. When I saw on the computers that you stole my money. *Mine!*" she roared.

"Where did you leave her body?" the male voice said.

Locust stepped closer. He grabbed her face. "Tell me now and you will live to see another day. We'll fill your account and ship you off, never to return again," Locust said.

"The bitch got in the way. Masterson, Cader, Sal, Merser, and Dolinth all wanted to fuck her. To make her their woman. They still do. That's why I stole all the money, even from them. She deserves to die. Everything was going fine until she was at that meeting. The bosses wanted her, too. She isn't better than me. I'm good. You know I'm fucking fantastic in bed, Locust. That bitch doesn't matter."

"Where did you leave her? Tell me now where her body is. Tell me now," Locust demanded.

Camille snorted, but then the men punched her again. She cried out as they tortured her, pulled back her fingers, and yanked her head back.

"What does it matter if she's dead, Camille? They want the body. You'll get that revenge you need knowing you killed their woman. Let them find her."

She stared at him. He nodded at his buddies. They released her, and she fell to her knees. "The shack in the boatyard, where all the trash belongs."

* * * *

Pelham heard the gunshot, and he saw red. They were standing by their SUVs around a parking lot not far from the old boatyard. "Keep Victor on standby, Costanza." Costanza nodded.

"Let's go," he ordered and got into the SUV with his brothers. Several vehicles pulled into the boatyard, and all Pelham kept thinking about was Melise and finding her dead body. Jordan was shaking, stretching his fists in and out, his eyes cold as ice, those of a killer. Carson and Warren had flashlights in hand and were shaking their legs, anticipating a search, and he knew they all feared what they might find.

As the SUV stopped and they quickly got out, they organized what teams would look where. "Every fucking nook and cranny. Every abandoned boat, car, dumpster," Pelham said, and they all headed out. It didn't take long to find the shack. Carson and Warren saw the electrical wires and antennae up on the roof of it and a makeshift line that led out toward the main road. They yanked open the door, and the sight had Jordan running and falling to the floor. Melise looked dead, her face bloody and battered, blood on the floor by her head, body limp.

"Melise. Melise, baby, come on, be alive," Jordan said to her as Carson gripped her wrist and felt it.

"A weak pulse, she's alive."

"Holy fuck," Pelham said, and they heard the others coming. "We found her. She's barely breathing, weak pulse," Pelham reported to Costanza.

"Get her to Victor. Go now, hurry. We'll follow. The guys will lead the way."

* * * *

Warren held her on his lap in the back of the SUV. Jordan was caressing her hair and staring at her battered face. "I can't lose her. She has to live," he said aloud.

"She'll pull through. She's strong," Carson said and swallowed hard.

"She didn't belong in the middle of this. She's so sweet, so naive. I knew that the moment I met her on the pier. I told her there were bad people out there. She didn't believe me. She took a chance on me, and I could have taken advantage of her."

"You didn't, though. You brought us all together. You helped to make her our woman, and she will be fine," Pelham said. The SUV came to a stop, and they quickly got out, then helped Carson to ease her from the backseat. They got her into what seemed like an abandoned warehouse and took the elevator upstairs. Their friends were there, and then the doctor appeared.

"Lay her on the table. Tell me what you know so far?" he asked, and they laid her down. She looked even worse.

"Save her, Victor," Jordan said to him, and Victor continued to attend to her injuries, and then asked them to leave the room.

Epilogue

Melise could feel her head throb, and she reached up to press fingers to her temples. She didn't want to stop painting. She felt so safe and at ease here at the estate. The beach was beautiful, the scenery around it stunning, and the house up above so glorious and old. One of the first ever built.

"Enough for today, baby. You don't want to be overtired or sick when your family and friends arrive," Jordan said to her, and then she felt his hands move to her shoulders before he dipped lower to kiss her neck and then her bare shoulder. She wore a plain white off the shoulder sundress and had a painting smock over it as precaution. She closed her eyes and exhaled.

"I'll need some medicine and then I'll be fine."

"You're pushing too much too soon. It's only been a month."

"I know, Jordan, but I love to paint and to be here with you guys. I can't just lay around all day and be catered to."

"Why the hell not?" Warren asked, joining them. She stood up, and Jordan unbuttoned the smock, and she pulled it off as Warren pulled her into his arms and kissed her tenderly. He was dressed up from some business meeting with Pelham and other men. Jordan had remained behind, and Carson was helping to set up for the small dinner party that wasn't so small. Warren released her lips, and then looked at her with his hand under her hair and head.

"You are so beautiful, my love."

She smiled, then reached up and stroked his jaw. "You are the beautiful one, Warren."

He chuckled. Jordan gave his brother and light punch on the arm.

"So sweet," he teased.

"Idiot," Warren replied, and they chuckled as they headed up toward the house. One of the guards she now had would bring up the painting and easel.

When they got to the pool area above, she heard the music, saw the tiki bar all set up, and Carson was wearing a Hawaiian shirt and khaki shorts. She smiled. "I love that," she said to him. He closed the space between them and hugged her to him as he nuzzled against her neck. She squeezed him tight.

"She's just coming up from the beach now? That's too long. How is your head?" Pelham asked, coming out to join them.

"It hurts. She needs ibuprofen," Jordan said.

"I have it here because I know she overdoes it," Pelham reprimanded, and then brought her the pills and some water. She took them.

"I don't overdo it," she said to him. He raised both eyebrows up at her.

"You do."

She pressed her palms to his chest and eased them up to his shoulders. "Maybe I need more discipline," she said, and his eyes darkened as his palm slid over her ass, squeezing it.

"Spankings are part of your discipline and training, yet it seems you enjoy them way too much," Pelham said, and she smiled.

"Well, your ideas of discipline are all pleasurable, so I think you have to think out of the box," she said, and then lifted up to kiss his lips.

He squeezed her to him and then held her in his arms as he released her lips. She rested her face against his chest.

"Your family is going to be here any minute, but know that I will be formulating a plan, and tonight you will be bound to the bed, and I expect you to accept whatever we dish out to you."

"Whatever you want, Pelham. I trust you," she said and looked at Carson and Warren. "I trust all of you and love you with all my heart."

They heard the voices, and Melise pulled back and looked toward the doorway. Her eyes widened as she saw her parents, her brothers, and Kiana between them.

"Oh my God, what is this?" she asked, hurrying to them.

Elliott pulled her into his arms and hugged her tight. "All your doing, Melise. You taught me that sometimes being stubborn and not taking chances could cause you to miss out on perfect opportunities."

"You mean Kiana?" she whispered.

"Like you took a chance on Jordan and his brothers, Kiana took a chance on me, Ben, and Phoenix. To think I was mad at you for texting her that day at the pier. Holy shit, I could kick myself," he said, and she laughed. He pulled back and she hugged her brothers, Kiana, and then her mom and dad. When she turned around, her men were there greeting everyone and smiling. Life sure was about taking chances, and the best one she took was opening up her heart to these four men.

THE END

WWW.DIXIELYNNDWYER.COM

Siren Publishing, Inc.
www.SirenPublishing.com

Lightning Source UK Ltd.
Milton Keynes UK
UKHW020617180419
341238UK00013B/1548/P